THE WOUNDED MIND

BY

STEPHEN HOWE

In loving memory of my dear late grandmother, Mrs Maud Mary Mills. The kindest person I have ever known, and who spent her life helping others.

I will never forget you and I will hold you in my heart forever.

Chapter One

Ridgeway Stables, Oxfordshire, 1914

The colt's flank shone a rich glossy black in the mid-morning sunlight that filtered through the planked roof and illuminated a river of dust. The horse's midnight hair was coarse under Frankie's palms as they brushed over him, the colt's muscles shivering at the firm touch. Even after all this time, Frankie still marvelled at the heat of the flesh and the pure, barely contained power of the magnificent beast.

'Good boy, Jackie.'

Frankie paused and closed his eyes momentarily; letting the earthy scents of the stable fill him. He loved the sharp reek of the manure, the sweet warmth of the freshly laid straw and the rich waxiness of the leather tack and the brass fittings that gleamed from his hard work. Everything he loved was here in Ridgeway, the horses, his friends and, of course, above all, Mary. Wherever she was would be his home and it had been the case since he had first laid eyes on her.

For a second, Frankie frowned; leaving this place, for however short a time, would be the hardest thing he would ever have to do. But what choice did he have? Young men

1

had a duty, and Frankie would not be found wanting.

'You dreaming again, lad?'

The voice was jovial, rich in country timbre, but its arrival was still unexpected and Frankie's eyes snapped open at the sudden interruption of his thoughts. He felt his face flushing with embarrassment. He caught sight of Jackie's long black face and, for a fleeting moment, he thought the deep, doe eyes were judging him, but that ended when a thick heavy hand slapped down painfully on his shoulder.

'Sorry, Fred,' Frankie stuttered. 'I was just lost in thought.'

The older trainer gave a fatherly squeeze to Frankie's shoulder and then pulled away.

'That's all right, lad. You've got a lot to think about. You taking Mary out for her surprise today?'

Frankie nodded. 'I hope so. Thank you for letting us have the afternoon off. I'll make it up to you, I promise.'

'Don't be daft, boy.' Fred grinned. 'You know me, an old romantic. Anything for young love.'

'Well, it really is appreciated,' Frankie said. 'Not just the afternoon off, but for everything you've done. Taking me in after my father passed, giving me a job until I came into my inheritance, helping me with all the legal papers. Thank you.'

Fred's jowls suddenly flushed a patchy crimson; he turned his face away and laughed weakly.

'Now don't you go getting all soppy on me, boy. Your old dad did me many a favour, and there was no way I'd leave you in the care of some step-uncle now, would I? Besides, now your money's come through, you're a wealthy man. You can be someone else's problem. Unless you want to stay, of course.'

'Thank you.'

'I said stop it,' laughed Fred. 'Now, you'd better be getting ready anyway. You're not taking Mary out in that awful new motorcar thing are you?'

'I have to,' replied Frankie. 'She's dying for a trip.'

'I dunno. You young folk spending their time around God's greatest creation, horses, and then the first thing you does when you come into some cash is go out and buy some smelly, clanking machine.' Fred's grin widened. 'Go on, boy. Off with you. Go get changed and take young Mary out. She deserves a break.'

Frankie smiled and took Fred's meaty hand into his own, giving it a squeeze before turning to leave.

'Oh, boy?' Fred called, his cheerful tone disappearing. 'Are you going to tell Mary about your other news?'

Frankie froze and nodded slowly.

'Good,' said Fred. 'The girl deserves to know. You're doing the right thing, but you need to tell her.'

***

The journey was another slice of heaven. The new car, resplendent in racing-green, roared along the narrow, green-roofed roads; Mary's beautiful, long, brown hair blowing in the wind.

'Not too fast, Frankie, please,' said Mary.

'Sorry,' said Frankie, taking his foot off the accelerator. 'I just wanted to see what she could do.'

Mary smiled back in response. 'Where are we headed?'

It was Frankie's turn to smile. 'You'll see.'

The destination, it turned out, was a set of iron gates open to a short driveway and culminating at a large Georgian house. A man in a grey overcoat and black bowler stood beside a small black car parked in front of the house. The gentleman held a silver pocket watch in one gloved hand, as if he had been waiting for someone who was late.

Frankie pulled the car to a halt and, dancing lightly around to the passenger's side, offered his hand to Mary.

'Why, thank you, chauffer,' said Mary with a smile. 'What a beautiful house. Oh, look at the roses under the windows.'

'Mr Mills?' asked the man in a slightly strained middleclass voice, the expression beneath his waxed pencil moustache conveying both annoyance and apparent disbelief.

'Yes,' replied Frankie, 'and this my fiancé, Mary Dearlove.' The man held out his hand and gently shook Mary's, saying he was pleased to meet her.

'I am Mr Greene of Langley, Smyth and Greene. My

apologies, I had believed our appointment was at four. Shall I show you to the door, sir?'

'Of course,' replied Frankie, a little abashed. 'Thank you.'

The man nodded and turned towards the house, giving Frankie chance to check his own watch to see it was only now five past the hour.

'Are we here to look at this house?' asked Mary in surprise. Frankie merely grinned in response.

'The house,' said the man in his strained nasal tone as he strode forward, 'Speen Moor Manor, was originally built in eighteen-twenty-four. As you are aware, Mr Mills, it has four bedrooms, a study with original oak panelling, a drawing room and large kitchen. In the rear, it has a cobbled yard with small stable and a paddock of half an acre. As you can see, it has rose bushes along both sides of the pillared entrance and beautiful garlands of wisteria hanging from its mellow walls. In the late spring, it will be replete with violet-blue flowers. It stands in one and a quarter acres in total, including the driveway, of course.'

'Thank you,' said Frankie.

The man reached into his coat and withdrew a collection of keys, which he handed to Frankie.

'Will you not be showing us inside?' asked Mary.

Mr Greene looked suddenly puzzled. 'Whatever for, madam? Mr Mills purchased the property over a week ago. I am simply here to hand over the keys.'

Mary turned towards Frankie, her face such a mask of

surprise that Frankie could not help but laugh.

'Surprise!'

***

'Wonderful,' said Frankie, looking out of the sash windows of the master bedroom and drinking in the views across the rolling fields. 'Look at the view, Mary.'

'It's a beautiful view to wake up to,' said Mary, smiling at Frankie. 'Did you really buy this house?'

'Lock, stock and barrel.' He turned towards Mary and cupped her cheek with his hand. 'I bought it for us.'

'For when we're married,' said Mary happily. Frankie's smile suddenly fell. 'That's right, isn't it?' Mary asked, puzzled by Frankie's drop in enthusiasm. Frankie let out a sigh and scratched his cheek nervously, a sign Mary knew meant he was upset.

'Actually, I was wondering if you might move in sooner, maybe Angela will stay with you too, to keep an eye on the place for me.'

'Why?' Mary sounded worried now. 'You'll be living here until we're married, won't you? Frankie?'

Frankie's heart was pounding, he could feel sweat pricking at his skin and his stomach was churning with fear. He had been dreading this moment, not even daring to think about what he might say.

'Frankie?'

'I've enlisted!' The words exploding out like a bullet from a gun. Mary recoiled as if she had been hit. 'Me, Stephen and Alfie, we've all signed up to the New Army.'

Mary stood in shocked silence, eyes wide, glancing around as if looking for an escape.

'I'm sorry, Mary. I had to. We all had to. But it'll be all right. We probably won't even see the Bosch. Alfie says the war will be over before we even get out of training.'

'Alfie?' Mary's voice was a croak. 'My brother, Alfie?'

'I couldn't stop him, Mary.'

'He's too young. He's only seventeen.'

'He'll be old enough once we're trained.' Frankie reached out and pulled an unresisting Mary into his arms. 'We had to enlist Mary, the thought of leaving you hurts so badly, but we had to. The country needs us.'

'More than me?'

'I'm sorry, Mary. I wanted you to have the house so you're safe. I didn't want to upset you. I just wanted to protect you. That's all I ever want.'

Mary sobbed into Frankie's chest as they stood holding each other tightly. Eventually Mary pulled back, her breath coming out hard.

'Just promise me you'll all be safe.'

Frankie leaned in and gently kissed her hot wet face.

'I promise,' he said softly. 'I love you.'

***

The Four Horseshoes, Oxfordshire, 1936

The funeral of Bob Greenough had been as sombre affair. Trainers, fellow jockeys and a whole multitude of people from the racing world had attended, dressed in their best black with their saddest, most downcast looks. Condolences had been given to Bob's widow, brave words to his young son, and praise-full thanks passed on to the vicar – everything was done according to the tradition.

> *Our next race is the prestigious King's Cup, a grade one handicap chase run over three and a quarter miles. The purse for this is two-thousand pounds to the winning horse. Due to the heavy ground, which is very soft today, and this thick fog, many of the runners have been withdrawn, leaving only four to contest this great race. Champion jockey, Frankie Mills, is to ride the favourite, Windsor Boy. Second favourite is Pond Close ridden by Bob Greenough. The third horse is Candy King ridden by Charlie Jones, and the*

outsider today is Captain Pat ridden by William Donoghue.

The wake was held afterwards at the local tavern, The Four Horseshoes. This ancient pub, smoky and sharp with the ingrained sent of centuries of stale beer, was where most of the local racing community drank and, as everyone agreed, a more fitting location would have been hard to find.

A toast was given by the deceased's best friend, John Welch, 'Here's to the best friend a man could have,' and on those words everyone raised their glasses and drank.

The fog is thick here today, a hard way to race. The four horses have cantered down to the start line. The flag is about to be raised, it's raised and away they go. They're approaching the first, they're over. It's now downhill to the second fence, and... and is that Candy King falling? Yes, it is, he's out, leaving just the three.

'Hi, Frankie, I thought that was you in the church.'

'Stephen!' said Frankie before emptying his glass. He smiled at his friend sadly. 'Quite a turnout.'

'Can I get you another one before I go?' asked Stephen.

'No, thanks,' replied Frankie, 'there's a queue a mile long.

Besides, I ought to get going too. It feels wrong being here given what happened.'

'It was the weather, Frankie, the fog. You mustn't blame yourself.'

Frankie shrugged, then he sighed and gazed down at the worn rugs covering the stone floor.

'How's the family?' asked Frankie, changing the subject.

'Everyone's fine, thanks,' replied Stephen. 'Angela would love to see you and Mary soon, catch up on old times, eh?'

Frankie nodded in a non-committal way and let out another sigh, glancing towards the group of men trying to get served at the bar. 'Yes, of course. Sometime soon.'

'Well, let's set a date soon, hey? Look, I'm sorry, Frankie, it's all an awful, awful business. I really must be going though,' said Stephen. 'I've got to pick the children up from school on the way home.'

Frankie suddenly gripped Stephen's arm. 'Thank you, Stephen, for everything. Do give my best wishes to Angela and I will see you again soon, Mary and me. We'd love to catch up.'

Stephen patted his hand. 'And soon!' he said as he turned to leave. 'And soon.'

The remaining two are passing the winning post on this the first circuit. Pond Close is leading Windsor Boy, which I suppose means

Captain Pat has fallen somewhere in the fog.
This truly is an awful day to race in.

Frankie walked to the bar, queued and ordered another whisky. The landlord returned with his drink and, to Frankie's surprise, also handed him a letter.

'What's this?' asked Frankie.

'I found it on the bar,' replied the landlord, 'and it's got your name on it.'

Frankie paid for his drink and took it and the letter to a table at the back of the room.

There's one horse coming out of the fog. Just one. It looks like – it's Frankie Mills on the favourite, Windsor Boy. He's won it unchallenged. Frankie Mills and Windsor Boy win the King's Cup!

Frankie lifted the battered envelope. A cheap plain white one. Intrigued, he opened it and pulled out a tattered piece of paper, barely able to read the scrawled, smudged writing inside.

Frankie Mills,

*I saw you strike Bob Greenough several
times around the head with your whip. You
caused him to fall and hit his head against
the wooden rail post. That broke his neck.
You did it. You killed him.*

*I've not gone to the police or told anyone
else what I saw you do that day, but I will
unless you pay me your share of the
winnings – five-hundred pounds.*

*This is not a negotiation, Mr Mills. I WILL
REPORT YOU. I will contact you about
where and when to deliver the money.*

A witness.

Frankie's blood ran cold as he deciphered the words.
Someone had witnessed him striking Bob Greenough with
his whip, causing him to fall from his horse and lose his life.
It had been an accident, it really had. Pond Close had been
leading Frankie's horse, Windsor Boy, as they had gone into
the fog again. Frankie could hardly see at that point,
everything a grainy grey blur; all he could hear was the
thunder of hooves and the announcer over the tannoy. As
they'd turned into the bend, Frankie realised Pond Close had
switched to the inside rail. With Windsor Boy moving across
to join the other horse, he had somehow drifted across to
his left, pinning Pond Close against the rail.

Bob Greenough had shouted angrily to Frankie to pull his
horse away and lashed out with his whip, striking Frankie
unexpectedly across the throat. It was instinct when Frankie

then turned to Bob and lashed out with his whip, striking Bob several times around the head. It was instinct, the need to protect himself from attack. And then Bob was falling from the saddle, tumbling in the fog. It was an accident. Frankie had never wanted to hurt anyone and he had certainly never meant to leave a wife widowed and a young boy without a father.

But who could have seen me? Frankie glanced nervously around the tavern to see if anyone was looking at him, desperate to get an idea about who the witness might be, maybe to explain himself. But there was no one looking; Frankie was a shadow. Rubbing at his cheek, Frankie quickly finished his drink and rushed home. He needed to think.

Chapter Two

Loos, France, 1915

Mud. Everywhere there was mud. Frankie had never seen so much filth in all his life, even the air smelled of it, heavy and cloying, like the essence of decay. His uniform felt like it was made of clay. The putties that bound his trousers around his boots would have been pottery if it wasn't for the stagnant rain water that constantly wetted them, making sure they stayed as heavy wet mud instead.

Frankie had been in the trenches for three days now and already the novelty of campaign life had thoroughly worn off. This sea of browns and reds that were the landscape was a far cry from the white canvas tents and barracks of the training camp. Back there it had been just exercises and drills. Hard days, for sure, but at least no one was trying to kill you. Not like here, not like here at all.

Frankie leaned back against the corrugated-iron panel that had been placed against the sandbag wall, and allowed himself to slump down onto the mud-covered wooden fire step. Bored and tired-looking men were doing the same up and down the trench. Some distance away, one side or the other started engaging in light shelling; a murderous living hell for those under fire but, as Frankie had quickly learned, just background noise most of the time. After the initial burst of terror and the first distant thuds, he put it out of his mind.

'Another fine day,' said Stephen, emerging bare-headed from the dugout. He too looked like some mud-creature, his greatcoat plastered, although his Lee-Enfield was clean. He ran a grimy hand through his filthy blond hair before covering it with his steel Brodie. 'I tell you, Frankie, when I get home I'm going to take a bath every day. I think I'll be washing every day for the next decade to get this lot off.' Stephen grimaced as a particularly mangy rat scurried past, seemingly unperturbed by all the suffering humans. 'And I'll get me a good wife too. One who'll keep a good, clean, rat-free house.'

Frankie smiled. 'Well, what about that Angela? The short-haired girl from Ridgeway. You know she's always had a thing for you, don't you?'

'Really?' Stephen looked surprised. 'I hadn't noticed. She is quite pretty.'

'She is,' Frankie agreed. He leaned backwards, stretching his tired and aching back muscles. 'She's friends with my Mary, you know. When we get leave, we'll go out for a drink together perhaps?'

'Like she's waiting for you,' sneered one of the other men suddenly. 'Mary'll be off marrying Fred's boy now you're out of the way.'

'You shut your mouth, Ernest Keep!' snapped Stephen. 'Keep it shut or else.'

'Or else what? What're you gonna do?' shouted Ernie, rising to his feet. Tall and built like a cart horse, he loomed over the shorter Stephen and Frankie, and his mouth was twisted into an ugly grin.

'What are we going to do, do you mean?' Frankie and Stephen glanced back towards the new voice to see Alfie had arrived and was now standing behind them with his strong arms crossed, two heavy hessian sacks resting on the duckboards at his feet. Although still young, Alfie could match Ernie in both height and breadth, and the two already knew each other well; Ernie and Alfie both worked at a neighbouring stable to Ridgeway.

'All I'm sayin' is this Mary of yours ain't gonna wait around for some short-arsed pretty boy who's likely to get killed first time he goes over the top.' Ernie glanced around at the men, some of whom were clearly enjoying the drama. 'Chances are she's knocking boots with the owner's son right now. After all, she's already got your house and car, ain't she?'

Furious, Frankie lunged forward, fists curled ready to strike, but Stephen grabbed him and held him back.

'Come on then,' laughed Ernie, raising his fists. 'Come on.'

'What in the blazes is going on here!' The voice was thin but surprisingly commanding, full of upper-class scorn and confidence. It emerged from the young Second Lieutenant Radly, a boy who although a little older than Alfie looked much younger, childlike almost with his pale, downy cheeks flushed a comical red. 'Private Keep, what are you doing? Private Dearlove, weren't you meant to be doling out the mail?'

The mention of mail was like magical command. In that instant, all threat evaporated and the men surged around Alfie to see if they'd been sent anything. Frankie's heart leapt as a letter was shoved into his hands by Alfie. From the neat handwriting and the faint scent of perfume, he knew its source without needing to open it. He was still breathing in the fragrance as Stephen pushed his way through to stand by his friend, a battered old tin, half-unwrapped of its brown paper, held in his hands.

'Rock cakes from Mum, fancy one?' Stephen asked. His eyes darted to the letter in Frankie's hand. 'Who's that from?'

'Mary.' Frankie smiled. 'It's a letter from Mary.'

***

Speen Moor Manor, Newbury, Berkshire, 1936

The front door closed with a heavy clunk.

'Is that you, dear?' Mary called from the kitchen.

'Yes,' replied Frankie as he hung his hat and coat on the stand by the door.

'How did it all go?' asked Mary. Frankie could hear a note of concern in her voice and knew she had been worrying about him. He steeled himself to reply, not wanting to share his worries about the letter.

'Well,' said Frankie, 'there were lots of people and he had a good send off. Stephen was there too and he sends you his best wishes.' Frankie stepped from the hallway into the study and sat down in his armchair by the fire.

'Are you all right, dear?' asked Mary as she walked into the room. 'You look as white as a ghost.'

'Yes, I'm fine,' replied Frankie. 'Just a bit tired.'

Mary gave him a sad smile. 'Such an awful business. That poor man. I'd be broken without you, Frankie.' She kissed him gently on the forehead.

Frankie nodded noncommittally. He raised a hand and brushed it against Mary's soft arm. *What would Mary think if she knew the truth*, he thought. *Damn that letter, damn that blackmailer.* He could feel his pulse racing again, panic building in his chest. He rubbed at his cheek. *What if the blackmailer asks for more money? There's nothing to stop him. Nothing to stop him from hurting us both.*

'Dinner's almost ready,' said Mary, walking back out towards the kitchen.

'It smells delicious.'

Frankie placed his head into his hands. The pressure and fear were churning inside. He could feel himself shaking, like he had when he had returned from the war. Back then, Mary had just held him until the terrors passed. She had spoken soft words, cradled him and loved him through it. He had felt so ashamed to be like that in front of her, but she had loved him and held him, and it passed. And with each day, each week, each month, the panic had lessoned.

Mary could not soothe this away because she could never

know what he had done. He would lose her, disgust her. He needed to protect her from this, he needed to protect them both. But what could he do? How could he make this disappear? He needed to scare the blackmailer. Needed to make him feel threatened. He needed to know who it was and make the blackmailer terrified of ever contacting them again. That's what he would do. Frankie would not be beaten; no, Frankie would attack instead.

Mary called Frankie into the dining room and placed his dinner in front of him, the rich savoury scents filling the room with comfort.

'I've been considering retiring for some time now,' said Frankie, 'and now this terrible thing has happened with Bob Greenough, I can't put you through that. I've made up my mind. What do you think about it, Mary?'

Mary smiled at him. She reached out and placed her soft, warm hand over his. 'Whatever you decide, dear. Although I can't say I'm sorry, especially after poor Bob.' She smiled at him and for a second she looked eighteen again. 'Besides, you did say three or four years ago you would retire at forty and now you're forty-two, so perhaps it's all for the best.'

***

The following morning, Frankie phoned his agent, Michael Winter, and told him he was retiring with immediate effect and he would not be riding again. Michael tried to convince Frankie to continue, but Frankie told him that due to his age and the tragic death of Bob Greenough he had made up his mind and his decision was final. Reluctantly, Michael said he would notify all concerned, including the press, and wished Frankie a happy retirement.

Later that day, the phone rang again.

'It's Stephen,' said Mary, handing over the Bakelite handset. Frankie took it with a gentle kiss to Mary's forehead.

'Stephen, lovely to hear from you.'

'I've just heard the news. Retirement? My God, Frankie, are you sure? You've never ridden better!'

'It's the Bob incident,' said Frankie. 'I can't do that to Mary, I just can't. I've risked enough and I won't risk losing her. Not for anything.'

'It's a damn shame, Frankie, but I can't argue with you.' Stephen paused for a second. 'Still, they say it's better to go out at the top. At least there's not going to be some young Henry taking your title.'

'Exactly!' Frankie replied. 'Going out as the champion. What could be better?'

'Well, in that case I think I'll congratulate you instead. Wish you a happy retirement,' said Stephen. 'And if you ever need to talk about the Bob incident, you know I'm always here.'

'Thanks, Stephen,' replied Frankie. 'I know I won't regret it. See you soon, Stephen. Thanks for calling.' Frankie hung up the phone.

Over the following days, Frankie was inundated with

bunches of flowers, cards and letters of congratulations from friends and well-wishers. Then, on the third day, a crumpled, cheap, white envelope arrived. With a gut-wrenching terror, Frankie instantly recognised the scrawled, smudged handwriting of the address, noting the local postmark. He scratched at his face for a second and then tore it open angrily.

> *Mr Mills,*
>
> *Go to Shaw graveyard tomorrow night at midnight, alone. Put the five-hundred pounds into a bag and place it behind the headstone of Bob Greenough's grave. Then leave. Do not look back.*
>
> *Do this and you will never hear from me again. Don't do it and you'll regret it, as will your pretty wife.*
>
> *The Witness.*

Furious, Frankie screwed up the letter and threw it onto the fire in his study. Stabbing it with the iron poker as it crispened and went black, bright red lines dancing over the edges. The woodsmoke smell of the room soured as the paper was consumed, the air suddenly smelling to Frankie of sulphur, of cordite, of mud and death. Smells of fear and fury and war.

No, Frankie would not be intimidated and he would not be

threatened. Frankie was a soldier. He had fought in the war and he had killed men who had threatened him then. He had killed with rifle and bayonet and club as he had defended his friends and family. He would defend them again if he had to and no filthy blackmailer would dare challenge him.

Enraged now, Frankie stormed over to his desk and wrenched open the drawer. The gun still lay where he had left it back in 1919, thrown down in a fit of sudden fear and panic when he had sworn he would never touch a weapon again. Well, that was a promise he would break to protect Mary and their life together. He lifted the heavy German Luger and inhaled the smell of oil and old iron, the smell of strength and defence. He pulled out the magazine to check that the bright, brass rounds were still inside and then he checked the mechanism. Fingers slipping comfortably into place over the trigger, too comfortably. Oh yes, the blackmailer would beg to live, he would beg and he would be made to never threaten Frankie again.

Frankie decided he would wait until the next day and then he would go to Shaw graveyard and have a reconnoitre of the perimeter, noting the entrances, the pinch points and escape routes. Then Frankie would decide where and when to confront the blackmailer.

***

Frankie felt a fatalistic calm as he tended his horse, Jennet, the next morning. It was like the calm before battle as men made themselves busy, distracting themselves from the terrors and dangers ahead. It was an odd sensation and, to his horror, Frankie felt like he had missed it. He filled a bucket with water and poured it into Jennet's trough. He then gave her some fresh hay and groomed her before closing up the doors and returning to the house.

'Hello,' called Mary as Frankie entered the house. 'It's such a lovely day outside. A lovely fresh winter's day.'

'It is, cold but bright,' said Frankie. He felt a sudden urge to hold her and swept Mary into his arms, kissing her. Mary giggled and blushed.

'What's gotten into you?'

'Let's go for a walk along the river and have lunch in town,' said Frankie. 'You and me. A retired couple enjoying the start of a long retirement together.'

'Oh, that would be lovely,' said Mary. 'When shall we go?'

'Now!' laughed Frankie. 'Let's go now.'

They walked slowly along the path to the riverside. Hand in hand, like a courting couple.

'The river's high,' said Mary.

'Yes,' said Frankie, 'it's all this rain we've had lately.'

They watched the swans sail by as they continued their walk along the winding path. Mary pointing out and naming the other birds and flowers as they went. She had always loved nature and her childlike enthusiasm for local wildlife still made Frankie's heart sing with love for this wonderful, caring woman.

They climbed the steps and walked over the bridge to the café, found a table looking out over the river and sat down. The waitress walked over to take their order. 'I'm going to have the shepherd's pie,' said Frankie. 'How about you, Mary?'

'I'm going to have the fish,' said Mary.

'Could we have a pot of tea for two as well, please?' said Frankie.

'Thank you,' said the waitress, 'I'll bring your tea shortly.'

Frankie gazed at his wife. Despite a few shallow lines and the occasional grey in her long, brown hair, she was still every inch the beautiful girl he had fallen in love with. Mary's smile faltered for a second, becoming wistful as she glanced across at a harassed-looking mother feeding buttered teacake to a small girl a few tables away. *Mary would have made a wonderful mother*, Frankie thought sadly. *She had deserved to have been*. He reached out and squeezed her hand, exchanging a loving smile of shared sadness.

Moments later, the girl returned with the tea and placed the tray on the table. 'The food will be about ten minutes,' she said and then she left.

Mary took the pot of tea and started pouring. Frankie was thinking about the graveyard and his plan to threaten the blackmailer. He was suddenly brought back to earth when Mary said, 'Oh, Frankie, look at the little moorhens,' nodding towards the window. Frankie smiled and drank his tea.

The waitress arrived and placed each plate in front of them.

'Looks nice,' said Mary.

'Enjoy your meal,' said the girl as she returned to the kitchen.

They finished their lunch and Frankie asked Mary if she would like dessert. Mary declined, telling him she had to watch her figure.

'I'll watch that,' said Frankie jokingly.

Mary laughed. 'You have one if you like?'

'No, I'm full,' said Frankie.

The waitress came over and Frankie asked for the bill. He paid the girl and gave her a nice tip. 'Thank you,' said the waitress, who took away the tray.

Frankie and Mary put on their coats and left. They returned by the same route they had come by, stopping at the graveyard.

'Let's pay our respects at Bob Greenough's grave', said Frankie, 'as you were unable to come to his funeral.'

'That's a nice thought,' said Mary. 'I would like to pay my respects to that poor man.'

The air was cold. The frosts of winter had already set in, dampening the smell of leaf litter, and even this late in the day their breath still clouded and steamed as they spoke. As they walked around the graveyard, Frankie noted the layout, knowing it would be dark when he next returned, but then he had done the same during the war. The old skills slipping back with unerring ease.

'Here it is,' said Frankie, pointing to a grave still covered in wilting, browning flowers.

'He was only thirty-six,' said Mary. 'Poor man.'

'Yes,' replied Frankie.

'He was married, wasn't he?' asked Mary.

'Yes, he was,' said Frankie, rubbing at his face; sharp pangs of guilt stabbing at his stomach, his pulse starting to rise again. Had it really been his fault? Maybe he deserved this punishment? No! Mary didn't and it was she who would suffer if word got out. She was an innocent, and he would protect her.

'Poor woman.' She squeezed Frankie's hand, perhaps mistaking his fear for grief. 'I couldn't ever be without you.'

They stayed for a moment, standing in respectful quiet, and then continued their walk home. The wind was starting to pick up, so Frankie took Mary's arm and they walked quickly back to the house. It started to spit with rain just as Frankie unlocked the door. 'I'll set the fire,' said Frankie.

'I'll quickly get the washing in,' said Mary. 'It should be dry, even with the chill.'

Frankie added some kindling wood to the paper and lit it. Mary soon joined Frankie in the study.

'Oh, that's better,' said Mary, enjoying the warmth being given off. Frankie put a couple of larger logs on and turned on the radio. They both sat listening in silence for a while, then Mary got up, picked up her sewing basket and returned to her chair.

'I've almost finished your scarf,' she said. She pulled out a part-finished garment and began knitting. Frankie smiled. Mary was quite fond of knitting scarves; this too was a hangover from the war, when she and Angela had knitted them for the troops.

They were listening to the weather forecast when Frankie said, 'Sounds like it's going to be a stormy night.'

'Yes, it does,' replied Mary. 'Perhaps you'd better check on Jennet and make sure the stable door is locked?'

'Yes, I will,' said Frankie.

Frankie opened the back door and saw it was now pouring down, so he grabbed his coat and held it above his head. The rain drummed noisily on the taut material as he ran down the worn back steps to the stable and checked the doors were securely closed.

The evening passed and at nine Mary said she would go up for a bath. While she was gone, Frankie went over the plan in his head. *I'll leave at eleven-thirty tonight with a bag containing nothing but newspapers*, he thought. *The pistol will be in my pocket and I will place the bag behind Bob's gravestone, as asked, and leave the graveyard by the same main entrance.*

I'm sure the blackmailer will be watching. Surely, he would then leave by the rear gate, because he would think I could be waiting at the main entrance. I will leave, but will quickly run around to the back gate and wait, in hiding. As he comes along the path, I will confront him. I will make him kneel in the wet mud and beg for his life. Make him beg until I'm sure he is too terrified to ever come near me again.

Frankie got up, took the Luger from his desk and checked it over again. He then returned the gun to the drawer and locked it. Frankie heard Mary coming back down the stairs, so he returned to his chair. 'I've done the washing up,' he said as Mary walked into the room.

'Thank you, dear.'

They both sat watching the fire die down as they finished their tea. After a while, Mary stood to go to bed.

'Are you coming, dear?'

Frankie shook his head. Sometimes, when the memories came back strongly, he would sit up for a while.

Mary smiled at him lovingly. 'Goodnight, dear.'

Frankie reached over and kissed Mary on the cheek, 'Goodnight, my love.'

Chapter Three

Loos, France, 1915

Chaos!

The air was torn apart with the roar of machine guns, the thump of artillery, the shouting of orders, the screams of the wounded and dying, and above it all the near-deafening pulsing of blood through his ears.

Frankie's terror was a tangible thing, a wall of fear that pushed back against his every step as he stumbled forward, his rifle gripped tightly and unfired in his trembling hands. The air stank of cordite and the pepper/pineapple tang of the chlorine gas hanging in the air. That damn gas was meant to have been the great smiting strike on the German lines, but a sudden wind had blown it back, leaving the British lines choking and dying instead. Those German machine guns who ought to have been silenced were instead relentless, bright flowers of death on the edge of the trenches, mowing down men in their hundreds and then moving on to the next like some biblical punishment.

'Steady boys, steady!' Radly called to his men, his youthful voice sounding even more childlike against the roaring storm of horror. 'We're almost there now, almost there.'

Fighting the urge to run away, Frankie willed his legs forward through the churned mud, not daring to look around to see if Alfie or Stephen were still alive and nearby. The pace was slow and measured, tortuous when every fibre of your body wants to escape. The smoke and dust limited how far ahead you could see, a test of trust, walking through this valley of death.

A sudden pain. Frankie looked down to see barbed wire sticking through his trousers. A gust of wind blowing away the smoke for a moment and revealing thickets of the deadly obstacle, undamaged and uncut by the bombardment of the heavy guns.

'Jesus help us,' Radly muttered, close enough for Frankie to hear. The young officer's face on the verge of tears.

'Shall we cut through it, sir?' Sergeant Clifford spoke calmly. The old veteran already had his wire cutters in hand.

'Get down!'

The scything hail of bullets was almost instant. Instinctively, Frankie threw himself to the ground, injuring his wrist as he did so, feeling the wind of the deadly missiles as they whipped just inches over his back. For what felt like hours, he lay there in terror as the deadly wave passed over him, until the screams and shouts of his dismembered unit cut through.

'Lieutenant Radly? Lieutenant?' It was Clifford's voice, still commanding, but with an edge of panic to it now that unnerved Frankie more than anything.

'Frankie, Frankie, are you okay?' It was Alfie. The young man sighed visibly as Frankie nodded and accepted a hand, pulling him to his feet.

Death had visited the company. Men, who just moments before had been whole and vital, were now torn apart. Some were screaming, others coldly silent. Sergeant Clifford was kneeling beside the broken body of the young lieutenant; he and Stephen were desperately applying tourniquets to the body.

'He's alive, but we need to get him back to the lines or to a stretcher bearer.' Clifford caught Alfie's eye. 'You, Dearlove, you're strong, carry him back to help and then get back here if you can. Take a couple of men with you. Mills and Sheehan.'

With a nod, Alfie stooped and lifted the wounded officer up into his arms. Without a word, he turned back towards the British lines, Frankie and Stephen following closely behind. They travelled back through a living hell. Men, dead and dying, littered the ground, calling for help, their mothers or just calling. Frankie dared not look at them, his thoughts instead on Mary, on how he needed to see her again, just one more time. The three men ran blindly, unsure of their direction, trusting instead the increasing sound of heavy guns and the receding chatter of the machine guns.

An explosion to the left heralded the return of machine-gun fire. Alfie dived forward at the sound, disappearing over the edge of a large crater. Frankie and Stephen followed quickly, sliding down the steep muddy sides where they paused, panting. Seconds later, a fourth man leapt over, tumbling, gasping and panting, barely recognisable under his thick coating of mud.

'What are you doing here, Ernie Keep? You're s'posed to be with the sergeant,' Alfie snapped, laying the lieutenant's still body down against the filthy side.

'You think I'm cutting through that wire to be killed by the Jerrys? Nah, not when I can help carry his lordship out, I'm not,' said Ernie, picking himself up. 'You checked if he's dead yet?'

Frankie looked at the lieutenant, recognising the slight rise and fall of his chest. 'He's breathing.'

'No, you idiot. Him.' Ernie pointed in the other direction.

The three other soldiers turned to see a grey mass at the other end of the crater. At first it looked like a mass of rags, until Frankie noticed the legs and boots of a German infantryman. He started to move towards him, but Alfie was quicker, crossing the water-pooled distance and unshouldering his rifle.

'Just a cor—'

The attack came out of nowhere; as Alfie leaned forward, the prone figure suddenly turned and fired two shots from a pistol point blank into Alfie's chest. In that moment, Frankie took in the terrified German's young face, recognised his frantic attempt to escape and felt a hatred like never before. As Alfie lurched back, staggering and falling against the crater wall, Frankie was up, his training kicking in as he fired one shot after another into the twitching body of the German soldier. As the empty magazine clicked, he dropped the rifle and ran over to his friend; Stephen was there already, cradling Alfie's lifeless head in his filthy hands.

'Alfie, Alfie!' screamed Frankie, but it was too late. To Frankie's horror, Mary's brother was already dead.

***

Speen Moor Manor, Newbury, 1936

At eleven-twenty, Frankie quietly climbed out of bed, picked up his clothes and tiptoed downstairs. He walked into the murky study, turned on the light and dressed. He then took the loaded gun from the drawer and put it into his coat pocket. He heard a noise upstairs and, heart pounding, he listened for a moment, praying he hadn't woken Mary. After a few seconds, all was still quiet and so he put on his hat and coat. He glanced at the old clock on the mantle and saw it said eleven-forty. He knew the walk just up the road and around the corner would take about fifteen minutes. He picked up a shopping bag, put in some newspapers for bulk and walked to the door, shutting it quietly behind him.

It was cold outside, although the rain had stopped at least. Frankie walked quietly along the road, his pulse racing at every noise and animal call. He remembered such journeys from the war, on reconnaissance, or a raid or some other operation; picking your way carefully, trying not to make a sound, and knowing that should he be spotted the flares would rise and all hell would break loose. Of course, there would be no flares tonight, no German machine guns or artillery, just two men, facing one another in a battle of threats. Frankie's hand slipped around the grip of the Luger; well, he had the advantage there, didn't he?

Frankie reached the gates of the graveyard at five minutes to midnight. The headstones, brighter than the inky blackness, looked almost like some strange fungi. He gradually made his way through the monuments, picking his way to Bob Greenough's grave and its offerings of decaying flowers. Carefully, his nerves wavering in protest at actually defying the letter, Frankie placed the bag behind the headstone, as instructed, and then, as conspicuously as possible, he returned to the entrance. It was time for the next part of the plan.

Frankie hurriedly rushed around the perimeter to the back gate of the graveyard. Crouching low, he picked his way back, squatted down behind one of the headstones and waited. Ten minutes passed, although it felt much longer, and Frankie was beginning to think the blackmailer must have left by the main entrance. Again, he felt the panic, the terror. What if the blackmailer had done that, what if he had taken the bag and simply left, what if Frankie had missed him? Would he awake to a police visit tomorrow? Would it be in the papers that he was a murderer? What would Mary do? Surely sweet, honest, loving Mary could not bear to be with such a creature as him. Frankie's breathing started to speed up, his limbs shaking violently. He couldn't bear it; he couldn't live with that. Suddenly, the Luger was in his hand, the dull muzzle pointed at him as he placed it against his temple. It would be so easy; it would all go away and Mary would be safe.

An abrupt noise stopped him. Frankie lowered the gun and glanced around. Footsteps, light on the ground; Frankie had survived over four years in France by noticing such subtle sounds. Gradually they were getting closer. Was the blackmailer trying to sneak up on him? No, no, that would not happen. Frankie's heart was pounding loud in his ears, adrenalin flooding his body. His enemy was out there and Frankie would not let him take everything that he and Mary had created.

Frankie looked out from behind the gravestone and saw the dark figure approaching where he was hiding. The blackmailer was stooping, trying to hide, and he had something in his hand, something long, something metallic that glinted at the end... a gun, he had a gun! Frankie leapt up, his weapon already aimed and he fired once, twice. The shot's ringing out like church bells in the muffled midnight air. The dark figure lurched back, arms flailing for a second, and then fell to the ground.

His body numb with fury and terror, Frankie slowly walked over to the body, still holding the smoking gun in his cold, shaking hand.

Chapter Four

Loos, France, 1915

'Pack his stuff up quick, lad. Get the job over and done; it's easier that way.' Sergeant Clifford's voice lingered in Frankie's ear as he laid out his friends few possessions. There wasn't much that would be sent back to Mary and her father; a few letters, a razor and mirror, a battered diary, a wallet, and a photo of the Dearloves in happier times.

Frankie lifted the photo, tracing the faces of the small family in their old-fashioned formal poses. Mary's parents were there, her mother already looking frail due to the sickness that would eventually take her; Alfie was in it, although he was still a boy, smiling despite the convention; and then there was Mary, fifteen or sixteen years old and already beautiful.

Seeing Mary's face twisted at Frankie's stomach. She was at home now, in their home with the wood panelling, or driving the car or meeting with a friend. Unaware her brother, her beloved Alfie, was dead. She wasn't alone in that, of course. The attack had been a disaster, thousands had been killed or maimed, and even those few breakthroughs that had been made were tenuous at best. So many killed for so little, including amongst his own company. Yet, for all of his lost friends, it was for Mary that

Frankie mourned. He ached for her, to hold her when she learned the awful news, to comfort her, to apologise for failing to protect Alfie, for failing to protect her.

'I can't believe he's gone,' said Stephen, trekking through the mud of the trench, carrying two mugs of dark soldiers' tea. 'Poor bugger.'

'Poor Mary,' replied Frankie, accepting the scolding drink and wrinkling his nose at the faint whiff of petrol that accompanied all of the water in the trenches. 'I can't bear to think how she'll feel.'

Stephen nodded sadly. 'Radly's still alive at least. Sarge says he'll likely be sent home to recover.'

'That's something, I suppose,' said Frankie, placing the photo back down on the pitiful pile. 'Wish we could all be so lucky. I'd give anything to be home with my Mary.'

'I know,' said Stephen. 'God help us all.' As he spoke the words, a sudden silence fell across the trenches, the pounding of the heavy guns falling deathly quiet. For just a fraction of a second, hope lit up in Frankie's heart.

'You don't think—'

He was cut off by the piercing call of whistles rolling across the trenches of the front line. Frankie shared a look with his friend.

'Poor sods.'

***

Shaw graveyard, Newbury, 1936

Hatred filled Frankie as he knelt down by the side of the figure. The man was wearing a large, worn greatcoat, much like the one Frankie used when tending to the horses. He had a woollen knitted scarf, wrapped around his neck and over his face, evidently to disguise his appearance. Fighting back disgust, Frankie reached out to pull back the scarf from the person's face; he would know who it was who had threatened him.

'Oh God, no!'

Frankie stumbled backwards, dropping the gun in panic.

'God, no, please God, no.'

He sat for a moment, heart racing, as terror overwhelmed him. It couldn't have been, it was a trick, a mistake, something other than what he thought he had seen. He needed to check, he needed to prove he was wrong. Fighting every urge in his body, Frankie crawled back to the corpse, to the now-exposed face. That face he knew better than any other.

Mary's face.

'Mary, oh Mary, what have I done? What have I done?' Tears rolled down his cheeks as he pulled her body up, hugging it tight against him. 'Oh God, no, please, no, no, no.'

And then Frankie wasn't holding Mary's body anymore. He was back on the path, facing his home, with the bag of papers in one hand, an umbrella in the other. He checked his pocket. The Luger was there. Had it been some vision, some hallucination?

No, his heart wrenched again as he saw the blood on his hands, registered the memory of arranging Mary's body, of picking up the gun, picking up the umbrella he had mistaken for a rifle, and then leaving Mary, his Mary, his beloved Mary, behind, back there in that cold, dark, empty graveyard.

Frankie turned to run back to the spot and then stopped. A realisation struck him. He couldn't go back. What if someone had heard the gunshots? There could be police there already. And the blackmailer too; had he seen? Or was it Mary? What was she doing at the graveyard? Was she in cahoots with the blackmailer, maybe? Could she even have been having an affair with him?

The very thought made him sick and Frankie threw up in the hedge, bent over and panting. As he stood upright, his thoughts suddenly seemed clear. He needed to know what had happened. He needed to find out why Mary had been there. If she really was with his blackmailer then it was he, not Frankie, who was responsible for Mary's death. Yes! It was his fault, and if Frankie were in prison then he could not stop him. Frankie had to cover up what he had done. He had to find out who was threatening him and bring him to justice first. Then, when it was all settled, he would confront what he had just done.

But what to do right now?

Frankie suddenly realised that the first thing he had to do was get rid of the gun. Running back to the house, he walked across to the stable. As he opened the door, Jennet walked up to him. Instinctively, Frankie patted her down the side of the neck and then walked over to a far corner of her stall. He prised up two of the heavy cobblestones that made up the stable floor. With his bare hands, he scraped out a small amount of the cold, long-packed earth and dropped the gun into the hole. He refilled it with the earth, then replaced the cobbles securely as if they had never been disturbed and covered the floor with straw. He scraped up a couple of Jennet's droppings and placed them over the area where the gun was buried, to deter anyone from searching just there. Frankie then said goodnight to Jennet and returned to his study.

Frankie put on his slippers and, hands shaking, poured himself a large whisky, spilling much of it on the cabinet. For a moment, he thought he heard a movement on the stairs, perhaps Mary coming down to check on him as she had done all these long years when the memories had been too much and he could not sleep. It was then that he burst into tears.

Sobbing, Frankie fought to get a grip of himself, to force his thoughts back into that clear state from the road. He wanted to try to understand why Mary could have been in the graveyard at that time. *She must have been having an affair with the blackmailer*, he thought. *Maybe they were going to disappear off together once they had the money. That must be it.* Yet he could not truly believe that his sweet, darling, loving Mary was going to take the money and leave him. He felt the tears coming back and he started to scratch at his face. No, no, he could not give in to that. He needed to focus. He needed to get his alibi arranged. If he was going to find out what was going on, then he needed to be above suspicion. It could only be a matter of time before the police knocked on his door.

My wife and I went to bed at around ten p.m., and I slept until you woke me, thought Frankie. *My wife was not in bed so I assumed she was in the bathroom or in the garden perhaps, until you told me otherwise. That's it, that's what I will say*. Frankie got up, drank the last of the whisky in the glass, then poured and drank another. Then he slowly walked up the stairs to the bathroom and washed himself. He hung up his clothes and climbed into bed, a bed he would never again share with his Mary.

*** *

Frankie woke and for a few blissful, brief seconds forgot what had happened. Then it hit him and he burst into tears, before fighting the emotions back. When at last he could control himself, he looked towards the clock, which said eight-fifteen, and realised the police had not called. Suddenly, he looked to his left, hoping to see Mary laid there and that everything had been a bad dream. But, no, there was no Mary and Frankie accepted it had all indeed been real.

I must do exactly what I would normally do, he thought. He dragged himself out of bed and pulled on his dressing gown and slippers and walked downstairs. Mary would normally have been there either cooking breakfast or lighting a fire, but of course she wasn't and she would never do so again. Frankie opened the back door to see if she was in the stable, but of course he knew she couldn't be. *But*, a cold, hard part of him thought, *this is what I would be doing if I didn't know about last night. Perhaps she went to the shop for something? No, I would be panicking.* So Frankie went to the phone to call the police and report Mary missing. *I wonder why the police haven't called*, he thought, hesitating. *Of course, if Mary hadn't any I.D. on her, they wouldn't know who she was. That must be it.*

'Hello, is that the police?' Frankie fought to keep the terror out of his voice.

'Yes, it is. How can I help you, sir?' replied an officer on the other end.

'I'd like to report a missing person.'

'Okay,' said the officer, 'can I have the name of the person and a description of them please.'

Frankie told the officer it was his wife, Mary, and gave a detailed description of her.

'What age would your wife be, sir?' asked the officer.

'Forty-two,' replied Frankie.

'Right,' said the policeman, 'and when was the last time you saw her, sir?'

'About ten p.m. last night, when we went to bed,' said Frankie.

'Have you searched the property, sir, in case she's fallen or something?'

'Yes,' said Frankie, starting to lose his temper. 'I've checked everywhere. Her coat and shoes are missing. I waited a while before phoning because I thought she may have gone to the shop.'

'Maybe that's exactly where she has gone,' said the officer.

'I'm sure she would've been back here by now and she would never have left without telling me. Please, I'm worried she may have had an accident or something.'

'Can I have your address, please?' asked the policeman. Frankie gave it and the officer replied, 'If you haven't heard from us by eight a.m. tomorrow morning, do phone us back. If, of course, your wife turns up, please phone us and let us know. In most such cases there is a perfectly logical answer, so don't worry too much. We will be in touch, Mr Mills.' Then the officer was gone.

Just for a moment, a boiling sense of guilt and horror welled up in him and Frankie again considered handing himself in and admitting to everything that had happened. *But if I did that*, thought Frankie, *the blackmailer, who is the cause of all this, would get off scot-free. I can't turn back the clock now, what's done is done. All I can do is somehow punish the blackmailer and end this whole nightmare, once and for all.*

What to do next? What would I do next? Get dressed, call for help. Frankie returned to his room, put on some old clothes, and went back to the phone to call Stephen.

'Stephen, it's Frankie.'

'Oh, hello, Frankie,' came the concerned voice. 'Are you well?'

'Not so good,' replied Frankie, the panic in his voice real. 'In fact, I'm really worried.'

'Oh, what's the matter?' asked Stephen.

'It's Mary,' said Frankie, 'we went to bed as usual last night and I woke this morning to find her gone. Her coat and shoes are missing, so she's definitely gone somewhere. That's why I'm phoning, I hoped maybe she'd come to yours?'

'No,' replied Stephen, 'she hasn't been here. Perhaps she's just gone shopping or something?'

'She wouldn't have gone without telling me,' said Frankie. 'Also, she normally makes up a fire if she rises before me, and no fire has been made.'

'That's strange,' replied Stephen. 'Have you phoned the police?'

'Yes,' replied Frankie, 'they're looking into it.'

'Okay, Frankie, I'm coming over. We'll find her, don't worry. I'll be there soon,' said Stephen and the phone went dead.

Chapter Five

Somme, France, 1916

The world was dead. All around Frankie was death, as far as he could see in all directions. No man's land was a hellscape of shattered and broken trees, of the rotting corpses of men and horses, thickets of barbed wire, and shell craters studding the blasted and torn ground.

A summer of horror had given way to a cold, lifeless winter of cold, wet and pain, and also a numbness, both of limb and spirit, that Frankie could not escape. It amazed him now, as he gazed out over the charnel ground he'd been ordered to watch over, that he had once been affected by death and suffering. He remembered the terror of his first conflict in Loos, the sense of loss he had experienced when friends had died, and even the empathy he had felt towards the dead and dying. All feeling was lost now, trapped beneath a self-made armour; corpses were just things, not people, and the new recruits were just corpses waiting to happen. Day and night was just an endless wheel of despair he could never escape. At least, not as a living thing.

Frankie stood up suddenly, both feet on the fire step so that his head emerged out from the protection of the trench. It was a stupid thing to do, they said, to show your head, at least if you wanted to live. Frankie was aware of at least four

German snipers out there, taking the occasional pot shot. If you wanted to live, you stayed down. If you wanted to live.

It felt odd, seeing the world beyond with his eyes rather than through the grimy glass of his periscope. The cold, frozen land of death seemed less real in reality. He noticed a corpse, some poor sod who'd been just like him once, lying just feet away, one arm outstretched as if grasping for safety. On a whim, Frankie reached for the hand, closing his own mittened palms against the slippery cold fingers of the body. He felt the tug of the corpse, as if he were pulling him out to join him, and Frankie felt powerless to resist.

'What in the hell are you doing?' Suddenly, Stephen was there, dragging him back, back from the frozen world of the dead. Back into the dubious safety of the trench. 'What's wrong with you, Frankie?'

Frankie glanced back blankly. 'I wanted to go out, Stephen. I wanted to go out there.'

'Don't be ridiculous,' snapped Stephen. 'If you did that, you'd die. And then what would Mary do?'

'Mary?'

'Yes, Mary.' Stephen was grinning now, although Frankie could not understand why. 'You've been granted leave, Frankie. You've been granted leave. You're going home to see Mary!'

***

Speen Moor Manor, Newbury, 1936

There was a knock at the door. *Must be Stephen*, Frankie thought. He took a deep breath to control his nerves and then walked to the door and opened it.

'Mr Frankie Mills?' asked a smartly dressed man in his fifties, grey hair battling with the black on his head and moustache.

'Yes,' replied Frankie. 'That's me.'

'I'm Police Inspector George Allen of the Berkshire force,' said the inspector.

'Oh, you'd better come in, Inspector,' said Frankie. As Frankie went to close the door, Stephen pulled up in his car. He paused to allow his friend time to exit.

'Any news?' asked Stephen as he walked up the steps to the door.

'Not yet,' said Frankie, 'but the police inspector is here.' Frankie ushered Stephen in and all three men walked into the study. Frankie noticed the inspector pausing to glance around and suddenly became conscious of the used whisky glass on the cabinet.

'Inspector, this is my friend, Stephen Sheehan,' said Frankie. 'I asked him to help me find Mary.'

'I think you'd better sit down, sir,' said the inspector. 'I'm afraid I have some bad news.'

'What's happened?' asked Frankie anxiously. He felt his body start to shake once more as he lowered himself into one of the heavy leather armchairs; the inspector taking the

47

other.

'At approximately eight-thirty a.m. this morning, the caretaker at Shaw graveyard, just up the road, discovered a women's body.'

'Oh no,' said Frankie, panic rising in his voice. 'It can't be her; it can't be. Not my Mary.'

'I'm afraid, sir,' said the inspector, 'the description you gave to the duty sergeant fits the person we found.'

Frankie began to cry, genuine tears; it suddenly felt real. Stephen put his hand on his friend's shoulder and said, 'It might not be her, Frankie.'

'I'm afraid I will have to ask you to accompany me to the morgue, sir, to identify the body,' said the inspector.

Stephen said, 'I'll come with you, Frankie.'

Trembling with shock, Frankie nodded and put on his shoes and took his coat from the hook. 'Okay, Inspector, I'm ready,' he stuttered. 'Please, let's go.'

The three of them climbed into the inspector's car and set off for the morgue.

The journey to the hospital was not long and the world outside was a crisp winter's day, the sort Mary had always loved. On arrival at the hospital, Frankie paused and took a deep breath and said, 'Please don't let it be Mary.'

The inspector led them through the building down a long corridor, filled with the pungent smells of disinfectant. When they reached the desk, the inspector informed the attendant of the body they wished to see, who then led them into a room where a corpse lay under a white sheet. The room was cloying with the pickle-like smell of formaldehyde and the flowery scents of detergent and polish, and under it all the all too familiar sickly sweetness of death.

'Are you okay, sir?' the inspector asked Frankie.

Frankie shook his head, unable to look at the familiar shape beneath the sheet. 'No, Inspector, I'm not. But, please, let's get it over with.'

The inspector nodded to the attendant, who pulled back the sheet to reveal Mary's face. She looked like she was sleeping, her long hair neatly tied back, her expression peaceful and her mouth almost smiling. But she was pale, deathly pale. Tears welled up again in Frankie's eyes; all he wanted to do was to kiss her, to beg for forgiveness. Still, he turned to the inspector and spluttered, 'Yes, it's Mary,' and then he began to sob.

Stephen put his arm around Frankie and said, 'I'm so sorry, Frankie.'

The inspector thanked the attendant and the three men left the room. As they walked back down the long corridor, the inspector turned to Frankie and said, 'I would like you to come back to the station and give a statement.'

'Don't you think he's been through enough already?' Stephen's voice was filled with emotion. 'Can't it wait until he's feeling up to it?'

'No, I'm afraid not, Mr Sheehan. You see, Mary was

murdered.'

'What?' said Frankie, tears streaming down his cheeks. 'You mean, she didn't kill herself?'

'No, I'm afraid not,' said the inspector. 'Tell me, Mr Mills, do you own a gun?'

'This is too much,' said Stephen. 'Frankie loved his wife and she loved him. Surely you can't suspect Frankie?'

'At the moment, sir, everyone is a suspect,' said the inspector.

'No,' said Frankie, 'I don't own a gun. After the war, I never wanted to see a gun again.'

'Of course, sir. I understand all too well.' The inspector gave a sad smile. 'However, you do understand we will need to search your house while you are giving a statement? Do you have any objections?'

'No', said Frankie, knowing they would only get a warrant if he did object.

They reached the police station and the three of them walked inside. The inspector showed them to his office and asked them to make themselves comfortable. 'Would you care for a tea?' he asked.

'Yes, thank you,' said Frankie. 'White with one sugar, please.'

'And you, Mr Sheehan?'

'The same,' said Stephen.

The inspector left the room and Stephen turned to Frankie.

'Frankie, I'm so sorry. Poor Mary. I don't understand why they are treating you like this, it's ridiculous.'

'It's okay,' said Frankie, 'They've got a job to do.'

'If it gets too much, just tell me,' said Stephen, gripping his friend's shoulder.

The inspector returned with another officer who sat at the desk ready to take Frankie's statement. An older lady came into the room carrying a tray with three cups of tea on it and placed it on the table.

'Thank you,' said the inspector and he closed the door behind her. 'I must caution you, Mr Mills, that anything you say may be used in evidence against you should it come to court. Would you like a solicitor present?'

'No,' replied Frankie, 'I've got nothing to hide. If I can give you any information to help find the monster who did this... well, I want to.'

'Very well,' said the inspector. 'Now, when was the last time you saw your wife?'

'At about ten p.m. last night, when we went to bed,' said Frankie. The other officer wrote it down as he spoke. 'I was a little later as I was struggling with some memories and needed to clear my mind. She was already asleep when I retired.'

'And you never woke during the night and found her not in bed?'

'No,' said Frankie.

'I have to ask this and I do apologise for the indelicacy,' said the inspector, 'but do you believe your wife was having an affair with anyone?'

'Absolutely not!' said Frankie. 'We loved each other very much.'

'Have you any idea what your wife may have been doing in Shaw graveyard late at night?'

'No,' said Frankie honestly, 'I'm totally perplexed by it.'

'Can you now tell me exactly what you did from the moment you woke this morning?' asked the inspector.

'I woke around eight-fifteen this morning and noticed that Mary was already up. I put on my dressing gown and slippers and walked downstairs. I went into the study expecting to see Mary making up a fire, which she would normally do if she was up before me. But she wasn't there and no fire had been made. So I went into the kitchen expecting to find her sat at the table, drinking a cup of tea, but she wasn't there either. I thought then she may have gone to the shop, as her shoes and coat were missing.

'I made myself a cup of tea and went back upstairs to wash and dress. When I came down and she still hadn't returned, I began to worry maybe she'd had an accident or something. Normally she would tell me if she was going out. That's when I phoned you,' said Frankie.

'And then Frankie phoned me, Inspector,' said Stephen, interrupting.

'And what did he say to you, Mr Sheehan?' asked the inspector.

'He just said he had woken to find Mary missing and was concerned for her because she wouldn't normally go off anywhere without letting him know. I told him to phone you and he said he already had. I said I would come straight over and help him find Mary, and that's when I pulled up in the car to find you already with Frankie.'

The inspector asked Frankie the same questions several times and Frankie kept replying that he had already told the inspector everything.

Suddenly, there was a knock at the door and a policeman called the inspector to step outside for a moment. He came back into the room and said, 'We have finished searching your property, sir, and no gun has been found.'

'I told you that,' said Frankie, 'and how did you get into my house when you haven't asked me for the key?'

'Well, sir,' replied the inspector, 'we used this one.' He showed Frankie a key. 'It was found in your wife's coat pocket.' He passed the key to Frankie and produced a small box from under his desk. 'You may want to take these, Mr Mills, it's your wife's wedding and engagement rings. The only other items found on her. It doesn't look like she was the victim of a robbery. Her clothes will be returned to you when forensics have finished with them.'

'Is that it, Inspector?' asked Stephen. 'I'd like to take Frankie home if you've finished.'

The inspector asked Frankie to read through the statement

he had given and to sign it if he was satisfied with it. Frankie quickly read the document through and signed it. The inspector told Frankie he could go but he was not to leave the country, and he would be wanting to talk to him again at some point. 'And believe me, sir, we will do everything in our power to find the person responsible for this.' The inspector offered out his hand.

'Thank you,' replied Frankie, taking the hand to shake. 'Please, please find the monster.'

The inspector motioned to a constable who led them out to a waiting police car.

They returned to a house that seemed cold and empty without Mary. Everywhere he looked Frankie could see her face.

'I think we could both do with a stiff drink,' said Stephen.

Frankie got out two glasses and poured two large whiskies, then passed one to Stephen.

'I can't believe it,' said Frankie, feeling the emotion rising again. 'Was it me? Was it my fault?'

'No, of course not, how could it be your fault?' said Stephen. 'Look, Frankie, you are in no fit state to be doing anything right now. How about I take you out for lunch somewhere?'

'I'm not really hungry,' Frankie replied.

'You've got to keep your strength up,' said Stephen. 'You need to look after yourself.'

'I think I might just have a lay down for a while after you've gone.'

'I'm not leaving you like this, Frankie.'

Frankie stood up. 'Please, Stephen. I think I just need some time alone. I need to be with my thoughts. I will call you and Angela later, I promise.'

'Oh, good God, Angela! How am I going to tell her about this? She'll be heartbroken,' said Stephen. 'Please make sure you do call us, Frankie. I need to know you are safe.'

'Thanks for coming with me today, Stephen,' said Frankie. 'I don't think I could have faced it alone.'

Frankie saw Stephen to his car and then returned to his chair. He sat back and thought through everything that had happened that morning. He opened his eyes and suddenly realised he must have nodded off. He looked at the clock and realised he had slept for over three hours because it was now almost four p.m. He got up out of his chair and walked to the back door, which was still locked. *How did they manage to search the stable when I've got the back door key?* he thought. He unlocked it, walked down the steps to the stable and opened the door and said 'hello' to Jennet. Frankie noticed straight away that nothing had been disturbed, even the droppings were still where Frankie had placed them. *Could it be the police didn't search the stable? Surely not*, he thought. *Maybe they didn't know about the stable.*

Frankie knew he could not risk having the gun found and would have to find somewhere else to dispose of it, in case the police returned for a more thorough search of the property. Frankie filled the water trough and gave Jennet some hay and walked back indoors. The sun was going down and the temperature was dropping, so Frankie went to the study and made up a fire and lit it. In the kitchen, he made himself a sandwich. *I suppose the next thing to do is collect the death certificate and arrange Mary's funeral*, he thought.

Frankie returned to the study, the room smelled of woodsmoke and whisky. Frankie felt lost, his eyes flickering to the doorway expecting to see Mary, smiling as she returned home. He was aching to hold her in his arms, to let out his fears and feel them soothed by her touch and voice. But that would never happen again. He poured himself yet another whisky, his eye's falling onto Mary's knitting basket on her chair where she had left it the night before. He felt like crying again, thinking of Mary saying she had almost finished his scarf she was knitting. With a sudden fury, he smashed the whisky into the grate and slipped down to the floor, overcome by his tears.

It was dark when Frankie opened his eyes again, the strange, logical calm had once more filled his mind. He felt tranquil, numb almost, even as he looked towards Mary's knitting. *Pack his stuff up quick, lad. Get the job over and done; it's easier that way.* The words were old, a long distant memory from when he was a different person. *Get the job over and done; it's easier that way.*

I must do something with Mary's things, Frankie agreed; Sarge had been right. He knew that to keep seeing Mary's things around the house was only going to upset him, that's why they had packed up the personal items during the war. It was the right thing to do, the only thing to do. Frankie walked around the study picking up everything that

56

belonged to Mary and took them upstairs and put them in one of the spare rooms. He then did the same with her coats and shoes and everything else downstairs, and put them all with the others. And, finally, he went into the bedroom, took her clothes from the wardrobe and laid them on the bed. He pulled out a drawer and added the contents to the pile. *Get the job over and done; it's easier that way.*

After Frankie pulled out the bottom drawer and emptied the contents onto the bed, he noticed the drawer wouldn't shut properly now. He took the drawer back out and looked inside to see what was preventing it from closing. Frankie stared into the space and saw something at the back, he reached in and pulled it out. It was a book, bound in cotton, and on the cover it read, *My Diary*.

Frankie sat down and opened the book up. The smells of lavender from the drawer and Mary's perfume filled his senses, and for a moment he was a young man again, reading the neat letters of his beloved whilst huddled in the trenches. Inside, Mary had written her name and the date she started, as organised in private as she had been in all things. For a second, Frankie traced a finger over the writing, drawing a connection with that wonderful, sweet soul. Then, curious, inevitable, Frankie began to read.

The diary was mostly about Mary's everyday life, mundane lists of meetings with friends and notes and fears about Frankie. He noticed Mary had written a capital 'N' on some pages and recognised the dates as those when his memories had affected him most, when the nightmares had taken hold in the night. Eventually he came to the last couple of pages and a note tore his heart in two.

*For some time now I have suspected
Frankie has been getting worse. Ever since
the accident he has been distant, his mind
drifting back to the war, going out for long
walks when he thinks me asleep. I admit to
have followed him on occasion, but it's only
to make sure he's safe. I couldn't bear for
something to happen to him.*

Frankie dropped the book, like it was suddenly red hot. *Oh, good God. That's why she was in the graveyard last night, she must have heard me get up and decided to follow me. She wanted to protect me and I... I...*

Frankie started to feel the panic rising, his breath becoming laboured. No! No, he needed to stay calm, to get the job done. If the police were to get their hands on this diary, he would become a suspect again. He couldn't let that happen; they could never know. At least, not until the blackmailer was punished. He had to destroy the diary.

Frankie hurried downstairs and began to throw kindling onto the fire until it roared back into life. He picked up the diary and held it to his nose, breathing in the sweet fragrances of his wife. Then, steeling himself and with eyes tightly closed, he tore the book into pieces, crumpled up the pages and tossed them into the fire so he wouldn't be tempted to read them again. He stabbed and stabbed them with the poker with all the fury of his loss until every trace was burnt and gone. The diary, like Mary, was now gone forever.

Chapter Six

Somme, France, 1916

It was hard to deny that the German trenches were better than the British ones, or at least those Frankie had experienced. They were drier and their bunkers more comfortable. Maybe it was their elevation that did it; certainly, that was Sarge's opinion. After all, it was hardly patriotic to credit the Bosch with anything other than being tough buggers to shift.

Frankie leaned back against the side of the newly captured position and took a breath of the cold, fetid air. The attack had been a success, a combination of artillery and guts really. By the time he and the company had made it to the Jerry lines, they were already running. Maybe half a dozen had stayed behind, putting up a fierce albeit futile defence with rifles and then raiding clubs, knives and bayonets. A very bloody and personal end.

It was the first victory Frankie had experienced.

A glint in the trench wall caught Frankie's eye. He leaned over and rubbed a thumb against it, revealing the barrel of a pistol sticking out of the mud. Frankie had no idea how it could have got itself buried like that, perhaps thrown by a shell blast or maybe it had been buried deliberately. Well, however it had gotten there, Frankie wanted it. Using his bayonet, Frankie carefully excavated the weapon, digging away at the heavy clay until it was free and he could clean the dirt from the grip plate with his finger.

'What've you got there, Mills?'

Frankie glanced up to see Sergeant Clifford standing a few feet from him, hand outstretched. Reluctantly, Frankie handed over his prize.

'Found it, Sarge. Just wondered how it got in there?'

Clifford smiled. 'It's a P08. Nice bit of engineering, even if it is Bosch.' He pulled out the magazine, inspected it, then tested the mechanism. 'Loaded and in working order. Good bit of kit this.'

The sergeant slapped the magazine back in place and handed it back to Frankie. 'Keep it safe, lad. You never know when it might come in handy.'

'Thank you,' said Frankie, a little surprised.

'Just don't let an officer see it though,' the sergeant winked. 'They might think you're a spy.'

***

Speen Moor Manor, Newbury, 1936

The following morning, Frankie phoned the undertaker and made the arrangements for Mary's funeral. It would be a simple affair, Frankie didn't believe in big showy funerals, not since the war. It would not go down well, of course; Mary had been popular in the community, always volunteering and helping out. Never having had the children she had craved, Mary had volunteered for various youth organisations and helped to organise the fete and the Christmas shows, anywhere she could direct her maternal energies. People would comment on the small service, the limited numbers of attendees, but Frankie didn't care. It was his memorial to Mary, not theirs.

Suddenly Frankie heard the sound of a car on the gravel driveway. He glanced out of the window and saw a police car coming up the drive. His heart began to pound again, his eye's darting around the room, suddenly aware of how suspicious it might look that all of Mary's belongings had been removed. His breathing began to get faster, sweat pricking at his brows. The diary! Frankie darted over to the cold fireplace. Fragments of burned and blackened paper filled the grate.

Damn it, he thought. There was no time to brush out the grate. *A fire!* Frankie grabbed a couple of logs off the stack and threw them onto the ashes, then tipped on all the strips of kindling.

There was a knock on the door.

Frankie grabbed his box of safety matches, lighting two at a time and tucking them into the kindling pile. One pair, two pairs, three pairs.

A second knock at the door. Frankie grabbed another four matches, lit them and hoped for the best before dashing to the front door.

It was Inspector George Allen, and the grizzled detective was smiling.

'Sorry, I was lighting the—' Frankie began.

'We've got him,' interrupted the inspector.

'What? Got who?' Frankie asked, taking a step back in surprise.

'The person we believe murdered your wife.'

Frankie felt himself flush. How was this possible? It had been an accident; how can they have arrested anyone?

'Who is it and why do you think he's the murderer?' asked Frankie, trying to control his panic.

'Well, sir, at approximately eight a.m. this morning, the caretaker of Shaw graveyard saw a man lurking in the trees at the far end of the graveyard. When he started to walk in the man's direction, the man disappeared. On arriving at the trees, the caretaker saw a homemade shelter and that's when he phoned us. We arrived ten minutes later and found the man inside the shelter. After a brief chat, we arrested him on suspicion of your wife's murder.'

'Good God!' Frankie scratched at his cheek. *What if the man had seen something... or perhaps... could he be the blackmailer?* 'Has he confessed?'

Inspector Allen shook his head. 'I questioned him back at the station and he denies any knowledge of the murder. He denies even hearing a gunshot on the night, although he was there and has been living in the woods for the last two months.'

'It still doesn't mean he's the murderer,' said Frankie. *Could he be the blackmailer? If it was him, then he'd deserve to take the blame.*

'No, that's true,' said the inspector, 'but when I asked him if he had a criminal record, he said, "I've never been in trouble with the police before." When we checked the records, we found he had a history of violence and robbery. And because of all these factors, we believe he is the man responsible. Of course, it will be up to a judge and jury to establish that. We will, of course, continue questioning him and hopefully get him to admit to the crime.'

'Oh…' Frankie replied flatly. *He has a history; he should be in prison. Is it so wrong if this bad man gets the blame?* 'Is there anything I can do?'

'No, that's it, Mr Mills. I thought I'd let you know straight away. And, of course, I will notify you immediately if there are any further developments.'

'Thank you, Inspector,' Frankie said, still struggling to comprehend what he had just been told. 'Thank you,' he repeated as the inspector walked back to his waiting car.

Frankie closed the door. *Can I let an innocent man take the blame for my crime? Is that wrong? But what if he was to hang? Would I have killed him too? But he's not innocent, the inspector said so. And he might be the blackmailer. I must phone Stephen and tell him what's happened.*

Frankie picked up the receiver and dialled the number.

'Hello,' said a women's voice.

'Hello, Angela?' asked Frankie.

'Yes,' said Angela. 'Frankie? Oh, Frankie, how are you? It's horrible, horrible what happened. Poor Mary. Poor, poor Mary.' She began to cry. Frankie felt his eyes tearing up to.

'Thank you, Angela. I'm sorry. I was wondering if Stephen was at home?'

'No, I'm afraid he's riding at Warwick today. Won't be back until this evening sometime. Can I help?'

Frankie could hear the pain in her voice. 'Okay. No, it's okay,' said Frankie. 'Could you tell him to phone me when he gets home? I have some news.'

'All right, of course,' said Angela. 'Are you all right, Frankie? Stephen and I are here if you need anything, you know.'

'Just about,' replied Frankie. 'Thank you. You've both been so kind.'

'We loved Mary too. Oh, Frankie, it's so horrible. You must be beside yourself. Please do take care of yourself and I will give Stephen your message as soon as he comes in,' said Angela, sniffing.

'I will. Thank you,' said Frankie and he put down the phone.

Frankie stood for a moment in silence, his eyes closed tightly shut and his head against the cold of the wall. Emotions of anger, guilt, grief and terror were all fighting for supremacy in his mind. He took a deep breath, forcing them back, trying to regain the cold, clear head that had taken charge before. What to do next? How to keep busy. *Of course. Clean out the stables, exercise Jennet. Stay busy!*

Frankie walked out of the back door and down the steps to the stable. For a moment he thought about digging up the gun, but then realised it would be a mistake to have it lying around until the night before Mary's funeral when he hoped to dispose of it once and for all. *I will dig it up a couple of hours before going to the graveyard*, he thought, *that will be the best thing to do*. He opened the stable door and breathed in the comforting smells of straw, manure, horse and leather he had known all of his life. Jennet looked up from her stall and Frankie reached out to give her a pat on the neck.

'You okay, Jennet?' he said, looking into her eyes. 'Just you and me now, girl.'

Frankie spent the next few hours keeping busy with stable work, his thoughts forcefully distracted from his sense of loss and guilt. When almost every conceivable job had been completed, he returned to the house. He was just relighting the fire and thinking about visiting the chapel of rest to say his last goodbye to Mary when the phone rang.

'Hello,' said Frankie.

'Hi, Frankie, it's Stephen. Angela gave me your message; what's happened?'

Frankie explained the inspector's visit.

'Well, certainly sounds like he could be the one,' said Stephen thoughtfully. 'By God, I hope the monster hangs for what he did.'

But should he? Frankie felt sick. *The inspector said he had a long criminal history. He is a bad person. Maybe he deserves to hang?*

'I've made all the arrangements for Mary's funeral,' said Frankie, quickly changing the subject. 'It will be at eleven-thirty on Friday.'

'Of course, Frankie. Angela and I will be there.'

'Thanks, Stephen. It's going to be small. You know.'

'Just those who need to be there. I know, Frankie.'

'Thank you,' said Frankie. He knew Stephen would understand. 'If you could be here for ten-forty-five that morning then we can all go together in my car.'

'All right, Frankie, we'll see you then. Take care.'

Stephen was gone and Frankie put down the phone. He poured himself a whisky and decided he would go to the chapel of rest the following morning to say goodbye to Mary. He got up and stoked the fire, then sat back down and thought about the blackmailer and what his next move might be.

If it wasn't the man they arrested and I was him, thought Frankie, *I'd still be trying to get the money. They probably think I intended to kill them that night and will be very careful about what they do next.* Frankie watched the dying fire for a while and then got up and went up the stairs to bed.

Chapter Seven

Somme, France, 1916

Dearest Mary,

Just a quick note to tell you how much I love you and miss you. It's been hot work here the last couple of days, but we are holding firm and doing our bit. Your letters are what keep me going though, my dearest. Each one makes me forget where I am for a few minutes. I remember that you are at home waiting for me and that thought will get me through this and home to you as soon as I can.

I am counting the days now until my leave and, I swear, I am like a child waiting for Christmas at the excitement of seeing you. It feels like our life before is so very far away and so very long ago.

I loved reading about all the work you are doing to make our house into a home, and I promise I will do everything in my power to come home to you safe and well. And when

I do, be sure I will hold you in my arms for an age. When this is all over and the world is whole again, I promise nothing will ever part us again.

I must be brief, my dearest, as I have more work to do. Thank you again for your parcels and do thank Angela too.

Stephen sends his love.

Always yours,

Frankie

***

Speen Moor Manor, Newbury, 1936

The following morning, Frankie rose at eight-forty, washed and shaved and then walked down the stairs in his dressing gown and slippers. He made up a fire and lit it. He went into the kitchen and put the kettle on to boil. The fire was burning brightly and Frankie stood in front of it warming himself for a moment, and then sat down in his chair and drank his tea. It still felt wrong, this routine without Mary there. Frankie wasn't sure he would ever get used to it, nor whether he wanted to.

Frankie dialled the undertaker's number, 'Hello, is that the chapel of rest?' he asked.

'Yes, it is,' came the reply.

'My name's Frankie Mills. I wonder if I could visit my wife, Mary Mills, today and say my last goodbyes?'

'Yes, of course, Mr Mills. Our condolences for your loss. We are open until four p.m.'

'Thank you,' replied Frankie. 'I will see you shortly. Goodbye.'

Frankie checked the fire had burned down and had a quick look around the house before putting on his hat and coat and walking to the door. He stepped out and shut it behind him. He climbed into the car, started the engine and off he drove.

On arriving at the undertakers, Frankie sat outside looking at the old-fashioned, black-painted shop. He had never thought he would be here, had always assumed he would die first. Never in all their years together had he ever thought he would ever let Mary down so badly; and now he was here, preparing to say goodbye to her. He wasn't sure whether he could do it, make that final statement. *No, I must, I owe it to her.* He scratched at his face as he fought to build up the courage, the strength to go through that door.

The little bell tinkled gently as Frankie forced himself through the black door.

'Hello,' he said to the lady behind the reception desk, 'I'm Frankie Mills and I've come to see my wife, Mary.'

'Certainly, Mr Mills. Would you like to take a seat? I will just prepare things and then you can go in.'

'Thank you,' said Frankie.

Five minutes later, the lady returned and asked Frankie to follow her. She opened a door to a room that was thick with floral scents and pointed to a pine coffin laid out in the centre. Frankie froze when he saw it, fear, grief and guilt fighting against the need to look upon Mary's face one last time. Pushing himself forward, he came closer. Mary looked serene, apparently sleeping in that quiet place. Her make-up applied as she had done it in life, serving also to make her seem less pale. It was almost as if she might open her beautiful eyes and smile at him at any moment, the way she had always done in the past but would never do again. Tears came to his eyes and he wiped them away with his hands.

'I'm so sorry, Mary,' he whispered, bending close to her body. 'I truly loved you.' He leaned closer and kissed Mary upon her cold forehead. 'Please forgive me and thank you for our life together.' He left the room and thanked the lady at reception. Outside the air tasted cold and sweet, but it was a relief from the heavy perfumes inside and all that they meant.

Frankie drove along the road to the park, where he sat in the car and looked across the river at the bench where he used to sit with Mary. He remembered how she liked to feed the swans, how she loved wildlife and could name every bird and plant, how she would collect wildflowers and press them, how they would gather wild fruits and bake together, how she had always been there to protect him, whenever the darkness, the memories, had resurfaced. It would never happen again. His angel was gone and Frankie would always be alone now. The rain started to fall and Frankie continued to sit and watch as it splashed against the water's surface. Until, with a sigh, he decided it was time to leave.

He started the car and drove slowly back to the house. Frankie pulled up, got out and ran up the steps and opened the door and stepped inside. He took off his hat and coat and shook them before hanging them up on the peg. He walked into the study where the fire was almost out and quickly put some more kindling wood on the dying embers and they soon burst into flames. He made some tea and walked into the study, picked up the whisky bottle and poured some into his cup. He turned on the radio and sat back in his chair.

He suddenly realised he hadn't informed the insurance company of Mary's death. He got up and looked through the bureau for the documents relating to Mary's life insurance policy. He finally found them under everything else and wrote down the telephone number on a piece of paper. He picked up the phone and called the insurers.

'Hello, my name is Frankie Mills and I would like to notify you of my wife's death.'

The man on the other end of the phone took Frankie's details and told him he would need identification and the death certificate when he came for his appointment. Frankie thanked the man and said goodbye. As soon as the man hung up the phone, Frankie called the coroner's office and arranged to collect the death certificate later that day.

Frankie walked out the backdoor to the stable and gave Jennet some fresh hay and a rub down. He went back into the house, checked the fire was almost out and put on his hat and coat. He walked out to the car and got in. He had decided he would have lunch in town and pick up the death certificate after. He drove back into the town and parked along the road from the café. He got out of the vehicle and strolled along the path and went in.

'Hello,' said the waitress, smiling sadly as she ushered Frankie to a table. 'I'm so sorry to hear about what happened to your wife. It's just awful such a thing could happen. She was a lovely lady.'

'Thank you.'

'Um... can I get you your usual?'

'Not today,' said Frankie. 'I think I'll have the roast beef and vegetables and a pot of tea, please.' The girl made a note and left for the kitchen.

A few minutes later, the waitress returned with Frankie's pot of tea. Frankie poured himself a cup and gazed at the window where Mary liked to sit so she could look out over the river. In his imagination, he could still see her there, smiling as she always had, chatting to friends as they passed and holding Frankie's hand when he felt strange.

'Here we are,' said the waitress, returning with Frankie's meal and breaking his thoughts. She put the plate in front of him and asked if he needed anything else.

'No, that's fine, thank you,' Frankie replied. The girl smiled and left Frankie to eat his meal. He ate slowly, mechanically, barely tasting it. Thoughts swirling in his mind.

After he had finished, he paid his bill and, as usual, left the waitress a nice tip.

'Thank you, sir,' the girl replied. 'Again, so sorry to hear your news.'

Frankie walked back along the road to the car and got in. He went over the route to the coroner's office in his mind and then set off. On arriving, Frankie rang the bell on the reception desk and a woman in a tweed suit came out of an office.

'Hello,' said the woman, 'how can I help?'

'Hello,' said Frankie, 'I've come to pick up my wife's death certificate.'

'What was her name, please?'

'Mary Mills,' replied Frankie. He showed the woman his identification and she gave him the certificate. 'Thank you very much,' said Frankie and he walked out of the door to his car and got in. That was it, Mary was now officially gone.

His next stop was at the insurers' office, an upmarket establishment located in a converted town house. Frankie remembered when he and Mary had first come here, not long after he had returned from the war. He hadn't intended to insure Mary, his plan was to ensure she was protected should something happen to him. It had been Mary's insistence that she also be covered.

'But nothing will hurt you,' Frankie had promised.

'You never know,' Mary had replied, squeezing his hand. 'Better safe than sorry.'

'I won't let anything hurt you though. I promise.'

So much for his promises.

Frankie tapped the brass knocker firmly. The door was

answered by a white-haired lady wearing a grey dress, her half-moon spectacles making her appear like she belonged in a different era.

'Hello,' said Frankie, 'my name is Frankie Mills and I have an appointment.'

'Hello, Mr Mills,' she croaked through a dry smile. 'Please come in and take a seat. Someone will be out to see you shortly.'

Frankie sat down by the window and picked up a newspaper from the table. He had just started reading it when the door opened and the lady returned.

'Mr Mills, please come with me. Mr Forrest will see you now.'

'Come in, Mr Mills,' said Mr Forrest as he was led into the office. It was a large room, panelled with dark wood and dressed with expensive furniture. A photograph of the king graced one wall, whilst the other was dominated by an oil painting of a racing horse, the other major creature insured by the company. Mr Forrest sat behind an expanse of polished mahogany. A large man with ruddy features and thin, black-dyed hair scraped into an unconvincing parting. 'Please do take a seat.'

Frankie did as he was asked and then produced a folio of relevant documents and the death certificate and handed them to the man.

'Such a terrible business, Mr Mills,' said the insurer, taking the papers. 'My deepest condolences. A terrible inditement of the world today, is it not? A terrible business.'

Frankie remained quiet as the man read through everything. He answered a couple of questions before the man smiled, signed a piece of paper, opened his drawer and placed it inside.

'Well, the good news is everything seems to be in order, Mr Mills,' Mr Forrest said cheerfully. 'I shall instruct our administrators to release the funds to your account within the next working week.'

'Thank you,' replied Frankie.

'Very sorry to hear of your loss,' said the man. 'Should you require any further assistance from us, do let us know.'

'Thank you,' repeated Frankie, standing up and shaking the man's hand. He left the office quickly, clutching a copy of the papers and still in disbelief that so important a life as his beloved Mary's could be summed up in such a short meeting and a payment to a bank account.

How can the sun shine without you? How can the birds sing or children play? I cannot bear it.

***

Frankie dreamed of Mary that night. She was alone in the dark, scared, calling for him and he could not find her however hard he looked. He woke up in a panic, looking for her in bed until he remembered. Then he lay awake, weeping, until he fell back to asleep again. The following morning, Frankie woke to see the sunlight shining into the room. *Looks like a bright day*, he thought, climbing out of bed. *Mary would have loved it.*

Frankie spent the morning keeping himself distracted with chores. He washed his clothes, hanging them out to dry, cleaned his best shoes and let Jennet out into the paddock behind the stable. He then retrieved the gun from its hiding place. It felt strange to hold the thing again, this device that had brought him such pain. He could barely bring himself to touch it, lifting it and dropping it into one of the hessian sacks used for animal feed. Frankie then replaced the cobbles as if they had not been disturbed, then washed his hands.

The weapon retrieved, Frankie returned to the house, carrying the sack up to his bedroom. He was too scared to leave it unattended. He took his best suit from the wardrobe and laid it out on the bed. Downstairs, he took the clothes brush from the drawer and then returned to the bedroom and began to give his suit jacket and trousers a thorough brushing. He put them back on a hanger ready for the funeral the following day and then sorted out some dark clothing to wear that night to the graveyard.

Frankie went back downstairs and put a couple of logs on the fire. He took down a glass and poured a small whisky into it, and then sat down in his chair, drank his whisky and fell fast asleep. By the time Frankie woke, a couple of hours had passed and it was beginning to get dark. *Oh! Jennet's still out in the paddock*, he thought. He opened the back door and rushed down the steps to the stable. He opened the stable doors and walked around the back to see Jennet stood at the gate. Frankie opened it, put the lead on Jennet and led her back along to the stable. He took off the lead, gave her a pat and shut the stable doors for the night.

Back inside the house, Frankie realised it was time for the news. He walked into the study, turned on the radio and sat down in his chair. He wondered why the blackmailer hadn't contacted him again. *Perhaps something has happened to him? Well, let's hope it has*, he thought.

The rest of the evening passed without incident and at eleven p.m. Frankie went upstairs and changed into the dark clothing he had prepared earlier. He wondered if he should drive or walk. *It's only fifteen minutes' walk after all*, he thought. *No, what if I was stopped and found with the gun. I will drive and hide the gun in my spare tyre*. Frankie pulled up the collar on his coat and pulled his hat down to partially cover his face. He placed the gun in his spare tyre and got in. He started the engine and drove away.

Seven or eight minutes later, Frankie pulled up at Shaw graveyard. He sat quietly, nervously, for a minute to see if anyone was around. It struck him that the last time he had been here in the dark, had been the night Mary had died. The night he had killed. He fought back the urge to dwell on his emotions, he had a mission to complete. Instead, Frankie took a deep breath, got out of his car and quietly closed the door. He took the gun from the tyre, removed it from the sack and dropped it into his pocket. The air was frosty, too cold to even smell. Even the few animals awake at this time of year were silent, as if the whole world had frozen solid. He walked carefully into the graveyard, but despite his efforts the crunch of his shoes on the path sounded loud against the silence and with every step Frankie expected to be attacked or discovered.

The freshly dug grave was covered by a tarpaulin, so newly cut even the frost hadn't painted its silver filigree on the dark soil. He pulled back the heavy canvas sheet and revealed the looming maw of the earth, black against the grey-green of the night-time grass. Frankie saw a small ladder resting on the ground with a spade dug into a mound of soil next to it, so he pulled it out and climbed down into the grave. He scraped a small hole into the heavy soil at one end, wiped the gun clean and placed it in the hole. He then refilled it with the soil and trampled it down so it appeared the same as the rest of the grave.

Frankie climbed out of the grave, put the spade back in the mound and carefully pulled the heavy canvas sheet back into place. His heart pounding, he looked around and listened for a minute, and then crunched his way back to the car.

Frankie slowly drove back to the house, parked and went inside. His hands were still shaking as he poured himself a double measure of fiery whisky. *Thank God that's over*, he thought. He finished his drink and then took off his shoes and placed them on a sheet of newspaper in front of the fire to be cleaned in the morning, ready for the funeral. Frankie walked upstairs and washed in the bathroom before setting his clock for seven-thirty a.m. He pulled back the sheets and climbed in. *It's good the gun is finally out of everyone's reach, back to the earth where it came from. Oh, how I wish I'd never found the damned thing,* he thought angrily, before he fell fast asleep and dreamed of Mary.

Chapter Eight

Somme, France, 1916

Rain is the only acceptable weather for a funeral. If Frankie had been feeling poetic he might have suggested the heavens were crying for the lost, but if that could be the case then in these dark times they would never stop weeping.

Sergeant Clifford was dead.

It had been a shell that had done for him, actually for him and three other poor sods who had simply been in the wrong place at the wrong time. Poor Sarge was coming out of the bunker when it had hit and he'd taken a piece of shrapnel through the helmet and into the skull. At least it had been instant. Frankie had certainly seen worse deaths, but it was not the heroic, fitting end the sergeant had deserved.

'Shut up, you big girl's blouse. No point crying over what's done now. Get it sorted, get me buried and get this damn war done.' That's what Sarge would have said, Frankie knew.

There were only four men at the funeral, a deputation from the company. Four men and the padre. It seemed the right number. Frankie could still remember his father's funeral, back when he was fifteen, and his step-mother's not long after. Both had been big affairs, all about the food and flowers and the public display of grief. He had hated them as a child, hated the false pity, the distant relatives there for the wake as much as to pay their last respects.

No, this seemed better, thought Frankie, *more right*. Four men who had all known and loved Sarge; solemn, respectful, here to witness the return of the body to the earth. When Frankie died, that's what he wanted, provided they could find his corpse in the aftermath of battle. He glanced up at the other four men and knew they were all thinking the same, recognising their own mortality as together they carefully lowered the coffin into the cold soil of the Somme.

＊＊＊

Spleen Moor Manor, Newbury, 1936

Frankie woke to the alarm clock ringing in his ears. He reached over and hit the button, turning off the annoying noise. Again, he had a fleeting moment where the world seemed normal and he wondered where Mary was, before reality hit and he burst into tears. Today was the dark day, the day to say goodbye to the one person he had loved more than anything else in his life. He pulled back the sheets and climbed out of bed and then pulled on his slippers and his dressing gown. He walked down the stairs, put the kettle on to boil and then wandered into the study to light the fire. The whole house seemed empty and cold, numb somehow, like all the colour and emotion had drained from it.

After dressing into some old clothes, Frankie walked back downstairs and picked up his shoes, he scraped off the dried mud outside the back door and polished them to a military shine. He took them back inside and put them by the door ready for later. *I suppose I ought to have some breakfast*, Frankie thought. *Although I really don't feel like any*. He decided it would probably be best to put something in his stomach, Mary would have wanted him to. How often in those early days after returning from France had she forced him to eat? How many days had she fussed over him when he was in a fog of despair or chatted to him incessantly when he couldn't bear to speak, or held him, tight and loving, when he couldn't stop the tears or the shakes. Mary had cared for him so tenderly and now he had to care for himself, for her memory. It was for her memory that he put two pieces of bread under the grill to make some toast. He checked it was done, turned off the grill and sat down to butter the slices.

After breakfast, Frankie felt a little better; the self-care made him feel closer to Mary and so he returned to the study and listened to the radio for a while. The fire gradually burned down and Frankie thought about putting another log on, but then remembered he would be going out soon. He went to the cupboard, pulled out a dustpan and brush and unlocked the front door. He walked down the steps to the car and pulled the keys from his pocket. He unlocked the door and began brushing the floor in the back of the car. Once he was happy with the result, he moved to the front. After he had finished, he went back inside where he filled a bucket with hot water and added some detergent, then picked up a large sponge from the boot of the car and began washing it down. By the time Frankie had finished, the car gleamed in the morning sunshine.

He walked back into the study and looked at the clock. Nine-twenty-three – still an hour and a quarter before Stephen and Angela were due to arrive. He was momentarily tempted to pour himself a whisky, but thought he had better keep a clear head for the funeral. He hadn't really given much thought as to whether to invite the Sheehan's back for a cup of tea or take them out to lunch at the café by the river. *I'll ask Stephen after the funeral and see what they would prefer to do.*

Better check on Jennet, Frankie thought. He opened the stable door and Jennet came over to him. 'Hello, old girl,' said Frankie, patting her down the side of the neck. He checked her food and water, gave her a sugar knob from his pocket and shut the door. He walked back up the steps and into the house.

Better start getting ready, he thought sadly. Frankie climbed up the stairs and washed his hands and face again. Back in the bedroom, Frankie took his best white shirt from the hanger and put it on. He pulled on his suit, picked the black tie from the rack and put it on. He then put a splash of musky aftershave on his face, Mary's favourite on him, and put on his jacket. He walked down the stairs, put on his shoes, and with the poker prodded the dying embers of the fire so it would be out before he left the house. Frankie looked in the mirror, took out his comb and ran it through his short, black hair.

There was a knock at the door and Frankie opened it.

'Hello, Frankie,' said Stephen 'How are you doing? Everything all right?'

'Yes,' said Frankie, inviting him and Angela into the house. 'Hello, Angela. Thanks for coming.'

'Hello, Frankie,' she said quietly. 'I wouldn't have missed this for anything. Do you feel okay?'

'Stomach's a bit upset,' Frankie said with a frown, 'but it's got to be done. I'm not quite sure what to do after the service, would you like to come back here or would you prefer to go to the riverside café for lunch?'

'Well,' said Stephen, 'as it's only going to be the three of us, Angela and I wondered if you'd like to come back with us for lunch at our house? We don't think you should be on your own afterwards.'

'That's very kind of you, I would love to come and spend a few hours with you both. I'm not sure I can cope with being alone... after.'

'That's what we'll do then,' said Stephen.

'Well, we had better make a move,' said Angela. 'Time's getting on.'

Frankie opened the front door and let Stephen and Angela out and then locked it behind him.

Ten minutes later, Frankie pulled up in the lane beside the ancient church. It was another cold day, the fog bathing the old stones so it appeared as if the whole church were wreathed in fallen cloud, the old spire disappearing into the downy white. The vicar was already standing in the entrance as the three approached, he greeted them gently and welcomed them into the building. The air smelled earthy, of musty books, candles, old carpet and, over it all, the faint aroma of sweet incense.

Mary's coffin was laid out at the other end of the church, bedecked with a bouquet of flowers. Frankie felt weak. He took a deep breath and walked down the aisle to a pew at the front. There were more people in the church than Frankie had expected, testament to her standing in the community. Frankie looked across the aisle and saw his elderly neighbours, Jack and Elizabeth Prior, and behind them, Fred Broadway, Frankie and Mary's old boss.

Fred rose from his pew and took Frankie's hand into his own. His hands, once plump, rough and leathery, were now papery and thin; his once florid face, now thin and gaunt.

'I'm so sorry, Frankie. So, so sorry. You two were made for one another. It breaks my heart to see this. Breaks my heart.'

Frankie thanked his old friend and they took their seats as the organ began to play 'Abide With Me'.

'Please stand,' said the vicar.

The congregation stood and started to sing the hymn.

Afterwards, the vicar began telling the story of Mary's life and Frankie gave a little sob. He took the handkerchief from his top pocket and wiped his eyes as he recalled their life together. They sang a second hymn, 'I Vow to Thee, My Country', and sat down. The vicar made his closing speech and the organist played 'Londonderry Air', Mary's favourite song.

The pallbearer's picked up Mary's coffin and waited for Frankie to lead them out to the grave. Frankie shuffled along with his head on his chest, tears welling up in his eyes. The vicar said a prayer at the graveside and the men lowered Mary's coffin into the ground. Frankie said his last goodbye and dropped a handful of earth down upon Mary's coffin. Stephen and Angela came forward and Angela dropped a small bouquet of flowers down onto the grave.

'Goodbye, Mary,' Angela said, her voice cracking.

Others came forward and said their goodbyes to Mary too. Frankie could no longer contain himself and he burst into tears. Stephen patted him on the shoulder and steered him away towards the car.

'Would you like me to drive?' asked Stephen.

'No, I'll be fine in a minute,' Frankie replied. He opened the back door and Stephen and Angela climbed in. Frankie walked around to the other side of the car and got in.

'Right, Frankie,' said Stephen, 'if you drive us back to your house, we'll take my car from there and I will bring you back afterwards.'

'Okay,' said Frankie, starting the car and driving off.

***

When they pulled up at Stephen and Angela's house, it had started to rain. Stephen said, 'You two sit here while I go and open the front door. There's no point in all of us getting wet.' Stephen opened his car door and ran across the drive to his front entrance. He pulled out a bunch of keys and let himself in. He came running back towards the car with an umbrella and opened the rear door so Angela could climb out under it. Stephen walked her to the door and she went in. He turned to go back for Frankie, but Frankie was right behind him.

Stephen shook the umbrella and stood it in the corner by the door.

'Think I'll use the bathroom,' said Frankie.

'You know where it is,' said Stephen.

When Frankie came back, Angela was in the kitchen cooking and Stephen was in the lounge sat by the fire.

'Would you like a whisky, Frankie, or just tea?'

'Whisky would be fine,' said Frankie.

Stephen poured Frankie's drink and then poured a small one for himself.

'I hope you're not drinking, Stephen?' came Angela's voice from the kitchen. 'You know you've got to drive Frankie back.'

'I'm only having one small one and that will be it,' said Stephen.

'In that case,' said Angela, 'you can pour me a nice glass of red wine, please, darling.'

Stephen took a bottle from the wine rack and uncorked it. He poured a large glass of the red liquid and took it into the kitchen for his wife.

Stephen walked back into the lounge and turned on the radio. 'Some music to help us relax,' he said. Frankie and Stephen talked about the weather and made polite conversation until Angela walked in smiling. 'What are you smiling for?' asked Stephen.

'Oh, it's the wine,' said Angela.

Stephen laughed and said to Frankie, 'She doesn't drink very often.'

'It's all on and cooking nicely,' Angela said. 'Has Stephen asked you about Christmas yet, Frankie?'

'No, I haven't yet,' said Stephen.

'Well, Frankie,' said Angela, 'Christmas is coming up and Stephen and I would love it if you would come to lunch with us all on Christmas Day. The children are always very happy to see you as well.'

Before Frankie had a chance to reply, Stephen said, 'I'd come and get you late morning and take you back, so you can have a drink and not worry about the driving.'

'It's a very kind offer,' said Frankie, 'but surely you'd rather be with your family on Christmas Day?'

'Well, we will be,' said Angela. 'You and Mary were our family too. It'll be like the old days. Do you remember? You had returned on leave, and Mary and I had just returned from Charmouth?'

Frankie nodded. In truth he did not want to remember those far off days, when he had been whole and Mary was young and full of hope. He wanted to forget, to hide from his past, to slide into a comfortable silent oblivion. But being with these friends made him feel closer to Mary somehow, it was the closest he could come to getting her back.

'A table for six. Three adults and three children,' said Stephen with forced jollity. 'Perfect.'

'Well, if I wouldn't be intruding then, thank you, I would like that very much,' said Frankie.

'Right, that's a date then,' said Stephen.

'Lovely, I am really looking forward to it. Would you set the table, darling?' Angela asked as she got up and walked back towards the kitchen. 'I will start serving up.'

Stephen went over to the sideboard and took out the cutlery from a drawer. He laid places for the three of them and then asked Frankie if he would like to take his seat at the table. Frankie took off his jacket and Stephen hung it up on a peg. Angela came in carrying two steaming plates of food and placed one in front of Frankie and one in front of Stephen.

'Shepherd's pie, my favourite,' said Frankie.

'Yes, I remembered. It's a recipe my mother used to cook. I hope you like it. I'll just get the gravy,' replied Angela.

'It smells absolutely wonderful,' said Frankie as Angela returned carrying a gravy boat and another plate of food. She placed the gravy down in front of Frankie.

'Help yourself,' she said with a smile, 'but make sure you leave room for dessert because I made apple pie too!'

Frankie's face fell for a second. Angela noticed and brought her hands up to her flushed cheeks.

'Oh, Frankie, I'm so sorry, that was Mary's favourite wasn't it. Oh… I'm so…' Her eyes filled with tears.

'It's okay,' said Frankie. 'Yes, Mary loved your apple pie. She always tried to make it like you do, but never quite got it. It will make me think of her. It would be nice to talk about her. I miss her terribly.'

'I remember the two of you picking the apples off your old tree,' said Stephen wistfully. 'Before we had the children. You had so many off that old thing. Do you remember Mary sending the two of us off, proffering your surplus to the local elderly like door-to-door salesmen?'

Frankie grinned at the memory. Mary hated the idea of waste when others were in need. He had loved that ingrained kindness in her.

'I hope you weren't selling them,' Angela replied. 'But I do remember the two of you ending up down the pub and Mary and I wondering what had become of you, only to discover you'd run into some old army friends.'

'Well, old soldiers need share our tales,' grinned Stephen. 'Besides, we'd worked up quite the thirst after all that work being good Samaritans.'

They carried on sharing memories of Mary, remembering the times she had made them laugh or her many acts of kindness. The simple conversation soothing Frankie's grief. It felt good to be with friends, talking simply and not thinking of murder or blackmail.

Eventually, they finished their dessert and Frankie volunteered to do the washing up. 'Absolutely not,' said Angela, 'you're the guest.' She picked up the empty dishes and returned them to the kitchen. Stephen got up from the table and walked over to the spirit cupboard. He pulled out a bottle of whisky and poured a large one into a glass and handed it to Frankie at the table.

'Cheers,' said Frankie. Angela poured herself another large glass of red wine and sat down at the table with Frankie. 'That was a wonderful meal, Angela, thank you,' said Frankie.

'My pleasure,' said Angela.

'When I take Frankie home, I'll pick up the children from school,' said Stephen.

'Thank you,' said Angela, 'that will save me a journey.' She caught Stephen eyeing the whisky bottle and said, 'You can have one when you come home and the driving is finished for the day.'

Stephen smiled and winked at Frankie. 'When you're ready, Frankie, we'll be on our way.'

Frankie swallowed the last drop from his glass and stood up. 'I'm ready when you are,' he said. 'Thank you again for a lovely meal, Angela, and I look forward to my visit at Christmas.'

'And we will look forward to seeing you,' replied Angela. 'Remember you are our family and we are here for you.'

The two men walked out onto the drive and climbed into Stephen's car. Angela waved from the door and Stephen tooted the horn as they pulled away and disappeared down the drive to the main road.

'I was wondering,' said Frankie, 'if Angela would like any of Mary's belongings before I give them away to a charity.'

'I really don't know,' said Stephen. 'I will ask her and get back to you, Frankie.'

'Okay,' said Frankie. 'Mary had some jewellery and I thought it would be nice if Angela had something to remember her by.'

The car pulled up outside Frankie's house and he thanked Stephen again for the lovely meal and said goodbye. Stephen waved to Frankie as he drove away and disappeared into the distance.

Frankie took the front door key from his pocket and opened the door. There were three letters on the mat. Frankie picked them up and walked into the study, sat down in his chair and opened his mail. The first two were the usual bills, but the third was from the blackmailer:

So you intended to murder me!

The price has now doubled to one-thousand pounds because of what you tried to do. After all, you have taken two lives now. And, to warn you in advance, I have already written a letter telling everything. This letter will be put into the hands of the police if anything should happen to me.

In two days' time, you will bring the money to the graveyard at midnight and leave the bag in the same place. If you do this, you

*will never hear from me again and your
secret will be safe.*

*I hope you have learned your lesson after
killing your wife in mistake for me. I am
sure you want this over as quickly as
possible. Do the right thing and it will be.*

The witness.

Frankie's heart was pounding; pure, cold fury flooding
through his veins. Mary was gone now; the blackmailer
couldn't hurt her any more. He poured himself a whisky as
his rage settled into a cold, deadly clarity. He knew now
what he must do. This monster had taken everything from
him and Frankie had nothing to lose now, nothing. *There is
only one way to end this so he can never tell anyone or come
back at a later date for more money and that is to kill him
and get the letter*, Frankie thought.

He finished his drink and proceeded to make a fire. Once the
fire was burning he went to the back door and unlocked it.
He quickly walked down the steps and across the yard to the
stable. He opened the doors and there was Jennet feeding.

'Hello, Jennet,' said Frankie. The horse raised her head,
looked at Frankie and then went back to feeding. Frankie
checked she had enough water and closed the doors for the
night.

Back in the house, Frankie dropped another log on the fire
and gave it a prod with the poker. *How can I find out where
the blackmailer lives? If I could somehow follow the*

blackmailer from the graveyard, I could find out. And then get the letter and kill him. Frankie drank his tea and pondered his next move. *If I were to arrive an hour early at the graveyard, I could put a chain and lock around the main gates forcing the blackmailer to use the back gate. In the event he came that route, it wouldn't matter,* Frankie thought. *I could put the bag behind the headstone as planned but put a letter inside instead of the money, to give me more time. I would then leave, drive out of the cul-de-sac and wait further up the main road for the blackmailer to leave by the same route. I could then follow him back to where he lives. But what could I put in the letter that would delay everything for a few days, giving me time to carry out my plan?*

Frankie suddenly thought of his late-wife Mary's life insurance. *That's it!* thought Frankie, *I'll ask he gives me seven days to raise the cash as I'm waiting for my wife's life insurance money to arrive in the next couple of days. Then I'll pay him the whole one-thousand pounds he wants. Yes, that's what I'll do. I'm sure he'll give me the seven days because he wants the money and he knows Mary is dead so there's life insurance money coming.*

Chapter Nine

Newbury, Berkshire, 1916

With a final hiss, the great black train pulled in at Newbury station. This normal place still feeling like some strange fantasy world as Frankie, dressed in his uniform, hefted his kit bag and climbed down from the carriage, heading towards the exit and the large market square. Here he paused for a moment, staring at the statue of Queen Victoria and the four lions surrounding her as if it were some strange artefact, at once both alien and familiar. How could it be that life was so normal here, so safe and secure, when just a few miles away in France, hell had come to the world?

A sudden bang shocked Frankie out of his thoughts. For a second, it was shellfire, the threat of sudden death so close to seeing Mary. Frankie spun around, reaching for the Lugar he had carried in his greatcoat pocket all the way from France, but it was only a delivery man pulling barrels down from his cart. The florid and brawny man tipped his hat towards Frankie, who quickly turned away so the shock and fear on his face would not be recognised for what it was.

Frankie continued on his walk down through the town and then out and along the river to Speen. As he climbed up the winter-bare hill and along the lane leading to the house, he found his heart racing at the prospect of seeing Mary, a mixture of excitement, apprehension and fear. How would she react? Would she blame him for Alfie's death? He certainly blamed himself.

The site of the house was like something from a dream. Only two days before, he had been surrounded by mud, shell-gutted buildings and khaki-clad men wrapped in bandages, and now he was here, back home, to this place he had bought for his and Mary's future. Frankie walked up to the gate, quietly lifted the latch and quickly walked around the side of the house. There, standing at the gate to the paddock, like some angelic vision, was his Mary, with her friend, Angela.

'Frankie!'

It was Angela who spoke first but, as Mary turned in surprise, Frankie was already running, his bag dropped carelessly. He swept Mary into his arms, pulling her slight frame tight into him, her arms squeezing back. He could feel her hot tears through his shirt, his own eyes wet and blurry.

'Frankie! Oh, Frankie,' cried Mary, pulling back and looking up at him. Frankie kissed her, long and slow, savouring the heat of her mouth, the softness of her lips. Eventually, he released her and turned to hug Angela.

'Welcome home,' said Angela.

'Thank you, Angela. It's wonderful to be home, and especially to see my beautiful Mary again.'

Mary was still in shock. 'Let's go into the house,' she said, taking Frankie's arm. 'How long are you home for?'

'Ten days,' replied Frankie. 'Ten glorious days.'

'So you're home for Christmas then?' asked Mary.

'Yes,' said Frankie, kissing her again. 'Yes, we get to have Christmas together.'

'I've got something to do back at the stables,' said Angela, grinning. 'Back in a couple of hours.'

Mary was too startled to reply.

'Are you hungry, Frankie. Would you like me to fix you something?'

'No, thanks,' said Frankie, 'but I would like to have a wash and change out of my uniform.'

Mary grinned. 'I can't believe you're home.' She pulled him into another embrace. 'I've missed you so much.'

A few minutes later, Frankie walked back down the stairs and into the study where Mary was sitting by the fire. The house smelled like home, the savoury scents of baking, the smell of polish and clothes and Mary's perfume; there was no metallic tang of blood, no sharp notes of explosives or sweet decay from corpses, it smelled of safety and Frankie could have wept.

'That's better,' he said, fighting back the tears and adjusting his now unfamiliar collar. 'So good to be out of uniform.'

The clothes hung on his reduced frame and Frankie realised he must have lost weight. Frankie saw from her expression that Mary was having exactly the same thought, although neither mentioned it aloud.

'Come and sit down and tell me all about the war,' said Mary.

Frankie sat down in his chair and looked sadly at Mary. 'I'd rather not talk about it, Mary, if you wouldn't mind. Not right now, at least. I want to forget all about that and hear everything about you. My darling, it has been hell without you.'

Mary smiled. 'For me too. Well then, let me tell you what's been happening here. Um… Well, first of all, as you suggested I invited Angela to come and live here with me. It's been company for us both and it got Angela out of that awful accommodation at the stables. I'm sure you remember what that was like.'

Frankie nodded as she spoke. He couldn't take his eyes off her face. Her voice was like music, a music he had been craving for so long, and he could never hear enough. Suddenly, he realised he was listening to the sounds rather than the words.

'And Angela has even been giving me driving lessons so I can drive now, Frankie, thanks to her.'

'My goodness, you are amazing,' Frankie said suddenly. He got up from the chair and pulled her into another kiss. 'My Mary, a driver; I should love to be chauffeured at some point. I doubt the king himself has so beautiful a driver.'

Mary blushed. She seemed to be struggling to build up courage.

'Is something wrong?' Frankie asked, suddenly nervous.

'No, not wrong,' said Mary. She shuffled uncomfortably. 'I was wondering... um... Frankie, do you think we should marry while you're home on leave?'

'Marry?' said Frankie, surprised. 'There is nothing I would rather do more. But I think... I think I would rather wait until after the war is over. Mary, I've seen such terrible things, such suffering, so many husbands killed. If I married you now, I'm not sure I could bear to leave you to go back. I cannot bear to have you widowed. Can you understand, Mary? I need to have that promise that when it's all over we can marry. So I can marry you and never leave your side again.'

'I love you,' Mary whispered.

'But what I am going to do,' said Frankie, 'is see my solicitor and arrange that you get everything in the event of my death. I need to know you'll be financially secure if anything should happen to me.'

'Oh, Frankie, please don't say that,' said Mary. 'It's awful being left here not knowing what's happening to you or if you will be returning to me.'

'I know,' said Frankie, 'but we must be realistic about these things. Let me protect you.'

'Let's go for a drive,' said Mary. 'I need to get out of this house for a little while.'

'All right,' said Frankie. 'And where is my driver taking me?'

'I'll decide as I'm driving along,' said Mary, laughing.

They walked out of the front door and Mary jumped straight into the driving seat, put the key in the ignition and started the car.

'Ready, Frankie?' asked Mary.

'Yes,' replied Frankie nervously.

Mary drove down the drive to the main road and stopped. She looked both ways before pulling out onto the main road and then she accelerated away. The car whizzed through the country lanes and Frankie turned to Mary and asked her to slow down. Mary laughed.

'What's so funny?' asked Frankie.

'It used to be me telling you to slow down, now it's you telling me,' said Mary, jokingly. Mary slowed the car down. 'Is that better, darling?'

Frankie nodded.

They drove along for a few more minutes before Mary pulled off the main road and drove along a leafy lane and over a bridge to a hamlet known as Hamstead Marshall. Mary pulled over into the White Hart Tavern and got out.

'Now there's a lovely sight,' said Mary, looking back down the lane to the river's edge.

'What a lovely spot,' replied Frankie. 'I don't think I've ever been here before.'

They walked into the tavern and ordered a drink and some sandwiches each. They took their drinks and food and, despite the winter's cold, wandered outside and sat at a table overlooking the river.

'How did you know about this place then, Mary?' asked Frankie.

'Well, I was out with Angela one day, having driving lessons, when we stumbled across it.'

'Well, it certainly is a lovely spot, even in December,' remarked Frankie.

***

Over the course of the next week, Frankie went to his solicitors and made out his will naming Mary as sole heir to his estate. He also went to visit Fred Broadway.

'The job as first jockey will still be waiting for you, Frankie, when you get back from the war,' Fred told him.

Christmas itself was bitter-sweet, falling so close to the end of his leave. Frankie, Mary and Angela were joined by Mary's father, frail from sickness as he was. Still, they swapped simple gifts and Mary cooked them their first Christmas dinner together. And in the evening, as Mary fell asleep against his chest listening to the radio together, Frankie realised he could not have had a better Christmas gift than simply being with her.

The leave passed too quickly. Too soon Mary was driving Frankie back to Newbury to catch the military train. Frankie felt sick at the thought of returning. He felt the tension and fear of the trenches returning, the overwhelming urge to run away and keep running so the war could never catch him.

'I hope the next time you come home, darling, it is for good. I don't think I can say goodbye to you like this again,' said Mary, her eyes heavy with tears.

Frankie held her in his arms and kissed her lovingly. 'I hope so too, Mary. But, however long it takes, I will come back. I promise.'

The train pulled into the station and Frankie said his last goodbye. Mary kissed him again and reminded him that she loved him and would be waiting for him to come home to her. Frankie boarded the train and shut the door.

'Come back to me, Frankie,' Mary shouted as the train pulled away from the platform. They waved to each other among the clouds of steam and then Mary was gone.

***

Spleen Moor Manor, Newbury, 1936

The next morning, Frankie was searching in the shed for a big chain he knew he had somewhere. Without any luck there, he went down into the cellar and found it hanging on a nail on the wall. He continued searching for a large padlock that would fit between the chain links but, after a while, Frankie decided he would have to go and buy a new one. He took the chain and put it in a bag, then carried it to the car and placed it in the boot. He drove off into town, pulling up outside the hardware store and taking the chain inside with him. He tried a couple of padlocks before he found the perfect one for the job. He laid the chain and the padlock and the key on the back seat ready for his trip to the graveyard.

Back at the house, Frankie opened the back door and walked across the yard to Jennet's stable. He opened both doors and led Jennet out and along the pathway to the frosty paddock. He gave her a few pats and then opened the gate and let her run off into the field. He stood watching her for a while and thought back fondly to when Mary would ride off across the moors on a Sunday morning, and then he walked back to the house.

Frankie walked into the study, made up a fire and turned on the radio. *I wonder what would happen to Jennet, when I'm no longer around?* he thought. *When I see Stephen next, I must ask him if he would look after Jennet if anything should happen to me. At least she would have a good home.*

It struck him suddenly that if he were to die there was no one else to leave his estate too. *I will leave some money to the injured jockey's fund*, he thought. *That would be the least I could do after what happened to Bob Greenough. I will take care of my funeral and everything in advance. The house and everything else, including Jennet, will be left to Stephen and Angela.*

Frankie felt much better when he woke the following

morning, filled with purpose. He sat up in bed and went over the day's agenda – solicitor and the will, then the graveyard with the chain. After dressing, he went downstairs and took a sheet of paper from his bureau in the study and started writing out his will. Whatever happened now, he would be ready for it. Like a soldier facing battle, he would go, knowing his affairs were in order and the people he loved would be protected.

He drove to the solicitor's office and parked outside. Frankie walked up to the reception desk and announced himself to the young woman sitting there.

'Just go in, Mr Mills,' the woman said, 'he is expecting you.'

Frankie opened the door and walked in.

'Hello, Mr Mills,' said the solicitor. 'Come in and take a seat. Now, what can I do for you today?'

'Well,' said Frankie, 'my wife has sadly passed away and I need to write a new will.'

'Oh, I'm sorry to hear that, Mr Mills.'

Frankie reached into his pocket and pulled out the sheet of paper with his wishes on it and passed it to the solicitor. After quickly reading it, the solicitor replied, 'Well, that seems straight forward enough, Mr Mills. I will get this made up and arrange for you to pop in another time to sign it and make it official.'

'Thank you very much,' said Frankie, rising from his chair. The solicitor showed Frankie out.

Back home, Frankie returned to his plan. It was time to write the letter.

> *I will pay you the money you are asking, but I am waiting for my late-wife's life insurance money to arrive in three to five days' time. In seven days, at the same hour, I will return to this spot and leave a bag containing the one-thousand pounds. I trust this will be acceptable. If you decide to report me before then, that is your choice, but it will mean you will get nothing.*
>
> *Have patience.*
>
> *FM*

Frankie put the letter in an envelope and grinned as he dropped it in a bag. He would have his revenge on the blackmailer, after all he had nothing to lose now.

***

The old carriage clock on the mantlepiece was one of the few things of Mary's that Frankie had kept. Frankie wasn't sure quite how old it was, antique certainly, as it had belonged to Mary's father and her grandfather before him. Perhaps it had been considered elegant in its day, but it now seemed utilitarian with its boxy shape and plain dials. It was the simplicity that Frankie liked about it. Today, though, it felt as if the single, thick hour hand seemed to be taking forever to rotate. Frankie was left waiting, and waiting meant dwelling, and dwelling could be dangerous for Frankie tonight. He couldn't risk letting grief or his rage overwhelm him. He needed to be thinking about something, needed to keep his mind busy until it was time to enact his plan.

Christmas is almost here, he thought suddenly, *and I have got to get Stephen and Angela's presents and gifts for their children*. He decided he would drive up to Reading in the morning and buy all their presents. *I need to know what the children have got already*, he thought, *I'll phone Angela and ask her for help, that'll keep me busy*. Frankie picked up the phone and dialled the Sheehan's number.

'Hello?'

'Hello, Angela,' Frankie replied.

'Oh, hello, Frankie, how are you? Stephen's been meaning to pop around.'

'I'm fine, thank you. Doing as well as can be expected, I suppose. I hope you don't mind my calling, but I was thinking about Christmas and wondering what you were buying the children?'

'Well, the boys want those pedal cars but they're quite dear so we—'

'I'll get them those then,' interrupted Frankie.

'Oh, no, you mustn't spend all that!'

'It's fine,' said Frankie. 'I've got Mary's life insurance money and she would want it spent on the boys; I certainly don't need it. You know how much she loved them. I decided I'm going to buy everyone something really nice with it, from Mary. Now, what about young Clare?'

'Well,' said Angela, pausing thoughtfully, 'you really don't need to, but that does sound like our dear Mary. Clare... well, like most seven-year-olds at the moment, she wants a pram with this new celebrity doll.'

'What doll is that then?' asked Frankie.

'She's the Shirley Temple doll,' said Angela. 'All the little girls are talking about her.'

'Okay,' said Frankie, 'a pram with the Shirley Temple doll in it. That takes care of the children, now how about you and Stephen?'

'Oh, please don't worry about us, Frankie. You're spending too much already. Stephen and I have a little something for you.'

'Mary would want this. Please let me, Angela. I want her money to go to the people she loved most. Your children are the children we never had, and you and Stephen are our only family. I think I know what you and Stephen would love and it would also be enjoyed by the children,' said Frankie.

'Well, you know what's best, but please do not spend all your money on us.'

'Thanks for your help,' said Frankie. 'I'm going into Reading tomorrow to buy all the presents.'

'Well, have a lovely time and enjoy yourself,' said Angela, 'and we will look forward to seeing you on Christmas Day.'

'See you then, Angela. Regards to Stephen. Bye.'

Feeling hungry, Frankie prepared himself ham, egg and chips for dinner. Satisfied he was full, he got up from the table and walked outside to the paddock. There was Jennet waiting at the gate, ready to come in. Frankie opened it and gave her a pat and walked her back to the stable. 'There you are, Jennet, back in the warm.' Frankie closed up the doors and walked back into the house.

In the study, Frankie put another log on the fire and poured himself a whisky. While he sat listening to the radio, it suddenly occurred to him that although he could get all the presents delivered to his house, he would still need to get the presents to the Sheehans on Christmas Day. They certainly would not all fit in Stephen's car and it was him that was picking Frankie up and driving him back to his house. What he would have to do was get Stephen to come and put the boys' pedal cars in his car and Frankie could then take Clare's pram and the radiogram in his. *Yes*, thought Frankie, *that's what we'll do*. Frankie gradually fell off to sleep as he often did after a few whiskies.

It was dark when Frankie opened his eyes and the fire was almost out. Frankie slowly got to his feet and put another log on the fire. It was time to act, and to his surprise, Frankie felt quite excited at the prospect.

Frankie walked upstairs and laid out his dark clothing ready for that night. Back downstairs he picked up the bag containing the letter and walked outside to the car. He put the bag on the back seat with the chain and padlock and shut the door. He walked around the car, checking all the tyres, and then walked back inside. *That's it, everything's ready*, he thought.

Frankie sat back down in his chair in the study. The fire was now burning brightly and Frankie got back to thinking about the plan for the night's venture. *I must remember to go back to the graveyard and take the chain and padlock off the main gate after I get back from the blackmailer's house*, thought Frankie. When the clock struck ten p.m., Frankie walked up the stairs and changed into his dark clothing. He walked into the bathroom and washed his face to wake himself up. He then walked back down the stairs and checked he had the padlock key in his pocket.

At ten-thirty, Frankie walked out of the front door and down the steps to the car. He climbed in and started the engine and slowly drove away from the house. As he approached the main gates at Shaw graveyard, he decided to drive past and park a hundred yards or so further up the road. Leaving the car, he retrieved the chain and padlock and walked back to the main gates, looked left and right down the road to make sure no one was coming and pushed the gates shut. He pulled the chain around both gates and closed the padlock. He checked in both directions again and swiftly walked back to his car. *That's that*, he thought, as he opened the door and climbed in. Frankie drove slowly back to his house and went inside.

Right, thought Frankie, *one hour to go and then I will drive to the back gate of the graveyard and take the bag with the letter in and leave it in the same place as last time.* He walked into the study and poured himself a large whisky, took a big gulp and sat down in his chair and waited. It seemed to take an eternity for eleven-forty to arrive, Mary's old clock moving slower than ever. Finally, Frankie got up from his chair and walked to the door. *This is it*, he thought excitedly. He went down the steps and opened the back door to the car. He checked the letter was in the bag and then slammed the door shut. Behind the wheel, he started the engine and drove nervously to the graveyard's back gate.

When he arrived, he took the bag from the back seat and closed the door, walking quietly through the winter's mist until he came to Bob Greenough's gravestone. For a moment, he felt the urge to visit Mary, but he wasn't convinced he wouldn't lose his nerve. He put the bag down behind it and quickly walked back to the car, slamming his door shut, just to make sure the blackmailer knew he was leaving. He started the engine, gave it a few revs and drove along, out of the cul-de-sac. He turned the corner, drove up the road for 60 or 70 yards and then parked up. Now, all he could do was wait and hope things went to plan.

Twenty minutes slowly passed and Frankie was beginning to think the blackmailer wasn't going to show, his nerve starting to fail. *I'll wait for one hour and if he doesn't turn up I'll go home*, he thought. Another fifteen minutes passed, when suddenly a light appeared back at the entrance to the cul-de-sac. The car turned in Frankie's direction, so he laid down in his seat to make it appear there was no one in the car when the other vehicle went by. The car passed and Frankie sat up in his seat and waited until the car was at least a hundred yards ahead. He turned the key and started after the speeding car.

Up the hill, Frankie almost lost sight of the other car but quickly found it again once they were on the straight. He followed for almost four miles, staying at a distance so he would not appear suspicious. When the car ahead indicated to turn right into a small trackway, Frankie drove straight past and pulled up a couple of hundred yards further on. He walked back along the road to the trackway and found it was pitch black. Only the moon allowed Frankie to see where he was going. He crept silently along until, after ten minutes, the track opened up into a clearing. There stood the car outside a small thatched cottage with a glow in the window.

At last, thought Frankie, *now I know where you live*. He recognised the little house, part of the estate owned by the racecourse. It made sense the blackmailer would be one of the racecourse staff. But which one and why he had been so determined to hurt Frankie?

Crouching low, Frankie crept up to the old building, keeping close to the walls so his shadow would be hidden. He inched towards the window, watching the silhouette of the man inside, going about his business. Frankie paused beneath the window. In that moment, he'd have given anything for his old trench periscope, but wishes were not going to solve this problem. Carefully, slowly, he peeked over the sill. The man was at his stove, heating something in a pan on the gas. He was big, both tall and broad, although it was muscle given over to fat; his head was bald and his ears emerged from his skull like mushrooms. For a moment, Frankie did not recognise him. But when the man turned, Frankie had to stop himself from gasping.

Deep within Frankie's chest an ancient flame of hatred burst into life; a hot rage, decades old, that burned away the last qualms Frankie had about taking the blackmailer's life. For a moment, Frankie considered doing the deed right then, but he thought better of it. He crept away from the house, back along the muddy track to the main road and back to his car. He slowly drove back to his house, stopping only to retrieve the chain and padlock at the church, and parked up for the night.

Back indoors, Frankie took off his hat and coat and hung them up. He walked into the study and poured himself a glass of whisky, which he knocked back and poured another. The mission had gone perfectly and Frankie now knew who would pay. *Of course, it was him. Of course, it was that beast. Ernie Keep.*

Chapter Ten

Ypres, Belgium, 1917

The thick stench of smoke was everywhere. It hung in the air like a ghost.

The little farm house had been a refuge to the British soldiers. The Janssens were a kind and welcoming family, although helpless to fight the Bosch. They had done all they could to protect the patrolling Tommys – fed them, let they sleep in the barn and plied them with the good, strong, local beer. But that kindness to the allies had not gone unnoticed it seemed, it had not gone unpunished.

The barn and farm house were now blackened ruins. The fires that had destroyed them had been doused by the heavy rains that washed the fields of Flanders and turned the trenches into rivers of mud. Thick mud, hard to dig in to, hard to carve out the five graves for the murdered family.

The Germans got the blame of course. Revenge on this patriotic family for helping their enemies. A bullet through each skull and then into the flame of their house. Not hot enough to destroy the bodies, but flames enough to cook, to burn them to charred and blackened mannequins. It was best to believe it had been the Germans, that's what Stephen, newly promoted to sergeant, had said. Even if

Ernie had always kept a lecherous eye on sweet Adalheida, the Janssens' pretty, young daughter. Even if Ernie's patrol, made up of the scum of the company, had returned drunk and excited to report the attack. Even if Ernie, now a corporal like Frankie, had acquired a new pocket watch and some silver spoons – stolen from a dead Jerry, or so he claimed.

'We can't prove it and it might be dangerous to accuse what we can't prove,' Stephen had whispered. 'We can't prove anything, yet.'

But it didn't stop Frankie from hating Ernie.

***

Spleen Moor Manor, Newbury, 1936

The next morning, Frankie groggily lifted his head from the pillow and realised he had a slight hangover from the whiskies he had drunk the night before, but he had needed them after he had realised who the blackmailer was. The night had been one of nightmares, dreams of the Janssens, of Ernie's other crimes, of the looting of corpses, the suspected torture of captured German soldiers and of other civilians who had died, all had been discovered by Ernie's boys. He had dreamed Mary had been taken by those scum, he had been unable to get her back and he had found her dead from a gunshot inflicted by Ernie, rather than him. The nightmares Mary had once soothed now included her, another crime to lay at Ernie's feet.

He slowly walked to the bathroom, holding his head as he did so, and filled the sink with water. He washed his face, which immediately brought him to his senses, and then he shaved. Back in the bedroom, he dressed and then walked downstairs. He filled the kettle and placed it softly on the stove to boil.

Frankie opened the stable doors and filled Jennet's trough with water and made sure she had plenty to eat. 'Morning, Jennet,' he said in feigned cheerfulness, patting her down the side of her neck. He kissed her on the cheek and closed up the doors.

Back inside, the kettle had boiled and Frankie made himself a hot drink. He sat at the kitchen table thinking about the day ahead. He needed to put the nightmares to one side. He needed to be normal today, to not be seeking revenge, but instead to just be Frankie. It had been a skill he had perfected during the war, to put aside the hatred and the terror, and to live in the simple pleasures of the moment. He had paid for it later, of course, and no-doubt would again, but it was enough for now. Today he was just Frankie. *Well, should be quite exciting*, he thought, *buying the Christmas presents for everyone*.

He got up and made himself some toast. *Always a good idea to get rid of a hangover*, he thought. As soon as he had finished eating, he began to feel better. He walked to the door, took down his hat and coat and put them on. He unlocked the front door and walked out to the car.

Frankie drove down the road and into town and pulled in at the garage. The attendant came out and asked Frankie how much he would like put in.

114

'Oh, fill her up, please, and could you check the oil as well?' Frankie asked.

'I'll do that, sir,' the man replied and he started to put the fuel into the car. Once he had filled the tank, he lifted the bonnet, pulled out the dipstick and wiped it on an oily cloth and then put it back in and pulled it out. 'Just needs a can, sir,' he said as he walked over to a stand and picked up a can of oil. He walked back over to the bonnet and poured it in. 'There we are, sir, all done.'

Frankie paid the man and set off for Reading. An hour later, Frankie pulled in to the Woolworths' car park. *Right, pedal cars, pram and a Shirley Temple doll*, thought Frankie, he turned to talk to Mary and then froze in shock. It took a minute to get over the sudden wave of grief that hit him then, the sudden realisation that he was doing this alone, that he would always be alone. Had he been talking to Mary on the journey? In truth, Frankie couldn't remember.

Mary had loved buying presents for the Sheehan's children. Unable to have her own, she had spoiled them, lavishing them with love and affection, to the point they had considered her a second mother. How would they cope with her not being there? Frankie felt a sudden guilt in the fact he hadn't even asked. He took a deep breath and scratched at his cheek; perhaps they would be too young to understand. He certainly hoped so.

He walked across the carpark and into the store. He made his way along to the toy department and started looking at the girls' prams.

'Anything in particular?' came a woman's voice, startling

Frankie.

'Well,' said Frankie, composing himself. 'I'm looking for a pram for a girl of seven and the celebrity doll named Shirley Temple.'

'Here's a lovely pram,' said the woman. Frankie asked her if it was the most expensive, 'No, it's not,' replied the woman.

'Can you show me which one is please?'

The woman walked along the aisle and stopped and pointed at the deluxe pram. 'That's the one there, expensive but it is beautiful,' she said.

'Oh, yes, it really is beautiful,' said Frankie. 'I'm sure she will love it. Now, about the doll.'

'I believe we are sold out of the doll,' said the woman. 'But I will go upstairs and see if we've had our new delivery.'

'Thank you,' said Frankie as the woman walked off into the distance. Frankie walked along to the next aisle and came to the boy's section. Tricycles, pedal cars, toy soldiers and all sorts of wonders for young boys. He picked out a red pedal car and a blue one for the twins. *I'm sure they'll love driving them around the garden*, he thought. *Mary would have loved that.*

'You're in luck!' said the woman, walking up to Frankie with the doll in her arms. 'We had a delivery last night and the new stock will be put on the shelves later today.'

'So this is the doll all the girls are talking about,' said Frankie.

'Yes,' said the woman, 'she's our best-ever selling doll.'

'Right,' said Frankie. 'I want these two pedal cars as well, please. One blue and one red. Can I arrange to have them all delivered to my home please?'

The woman totalled up the bill and Frankie paid the money and got a receipt. 'Thank you,' said Frankie and gave the woman his address so everything could be delivered. As he turned to leave, he said, 'Oh, I don't suppose you'd know where I can buy the new Bakelite radiogram from would you?'

'Well, sir, the best shop in town for musical things is about two-hundred yards down on this side. You can't miss it,' said the assistant.

'Okay, thanks again,' said Frankie, walking back to the entrance.

He walked around the building to the main street and then down the road towards the music store, looking in the windows as he went. After a few minutes, Frankie came to a large showroom with musical instruments in the front window. *This must be it*, he thought and he went in.

'Hello,' said the shop assistant, 'can I help you, sir?'

'I'm looking for the new Bakelite radiogram,' said Frankie.

'Radiograms are upstairs, sir.'

'Thanks,' said Frankie and he walked up the steps to the next level.

Upstairs the whole floor was covered in a variety of radiograms and other musical equipment. Frankie had just started browsing when a young man in a blue suit came up to him and asked if he could help.

'I'm looking for the new Bakelite radiogram,' said Frankie.

'Ah, yes, over this way, sir.' The man led Frankie through the maze of goods and suddenly stopped and pointed. 'There it is, sir. The latest model and top of the range.'

'Wow,' said Frankie, 'that looks impressive.'

'It is, sir. Let me show you what it can do.' The assistant went through the various features and controls of the top of the range radiogram, eager to make a sale.

Frankie was hooked. *I'd really like one myself*, he thought. 'I'll take two!' he said and the assistant's face lit up.

'Yes, sir!'

'Can I have them delivered, please?'

'Certainly, sir!' said the assistant. 'Next day delivery?'

'Perfect,' said Frankie, taking his wallet from his coat pocket. 'I don't suppose you offer gift wrapping too?'

'I can arrange that, sir. Are they Christmas gifts?'

'Yes, please, but just on the one, please. The other is for me. I'm treating myself.'

'Yes, sir,' said the man.

Frankie paid the assistant and said 'goodbye'.

Back in the car, Frankie was feeling really pleased with himself at getting the presents he wanted. *Almost time for lunch*, he thought. *I'll pop in to the riverside café and have some lunch there when I get back to Newbury.*

It was raining when Frankie climbed out of the car at the café car park. He was just locking the door when he heard the distant scream of a women's voice shouting 'HELP', over and over. Frankie's heart started to race. He looked around and then ran in the direction of the distressed voice. About two-hundred yards away, he saw a blonde-haired lady shouting from the opposite bank.

'MY BOY!' she shouted, pointing to the river.

Frankie looked along the swirling river and could see a head bobbing up and down in the fast-flowing current. He ran as fast as he could along the bank until he had got ahead of the boy. He threw off his hat and coat and dived straight into the water. The impact stabbed him with a dozen needles of ice, stealing his breath and turning his limbs to lead. Frankie could feel himself being dragged down, could feel the panic rising in his chest, but he willed it back down, regaining control over his body.

Painfully, Frankie swam out into the middle of the river and grabbed the boy as he came rushing past. He put his arm under the boy's arms and pulled his head up out of the water. Frankie had trained in life-saving as a sea cadet, so knew exactly what to do. He laid back, pulled the boy up against his chest and began swimming with one arm to the far bank where a group of people had gathered. He lifted the boy's limp body out of the water and passed him to one of the men knelt down on the edge of the bank. The man carried the boy across to the grass and laid him down. The boy's mother screamed when she saw her son's pale face and lifeless body.

Frankie climbed out of the icy water, shivering, and rushed to the boy's side. He interlocked his hands and began giving the boy heart massage, counting as he went. He administered mouth-to-mouth resuscitation, but still the boy showed no signs of life. His mother was sobbing uncontrollably and begged Frankie to save her son. Frankie went back to the heart massage, again counting as he went. Two other men came running up and one started taking photographs.

'What's happened?' they asked.

'My boy fell in and this brave man dived in to save him,' said the mother.

One of the women whispered to another, 'he's gone'.

Frankie returned to the mouth-to-mouth resuscitation and then, suddenly, the boy spluttered, threw up, and opened his eyes.

'Bobby, Bobby,' the mother cried, wrapping her arms around the shivering boy.

'I know you,' said the man with the camera. 'You're Frankie Mills, the jockey. I took your photo at the racecourse last month when you won the King's Cup. My name's James Corderoy and I'm from the *Newbury News*. This is my colleague, John Endle.'

Frankie noticed the woman was looking at him sadly. *Perhaps she has heard about Mary?*

'I don't want any fuss,' said Frankie, shivering, his body

plastered in his sodden clothes. 'I just did what anyone would do in the same circumstances.'

'You are a hero, Mr Mills,' said the boy's mother, standing behind him with her son.

Frankie turned to the boy, who was now standing next to him, and put his arm around the little boy's back and pulled him toward him.

The boy turned to Frankie and said, 'You saved me, mister,' and put his arm around Frankie's neck. The photographer snapped away with his camera and the crowd clapped at the spectacle.

'We must get this boy home as quickly as possible and put him in a hot bath,' said Frankie. 'Do you have a car?'

'No,' replied the mother. 'We only live ten minutes' walk away.'

'Very well, I will take you both straight home in my car,' said Frankie. He picked the boy up in his arms and carried him along the riverbank and across the bridge to where his car was parked. He opened the back door and asked the woman to get in, and then laid the boy across the seat with his head resting on his mother's lap. 'I'll just run back and get my hat and coat where I took them off. I'll be straight back,' he said as he closed the car door.

Frankie ran back across the carpark to the near riverbank and picked up his hat and coat and returned to the car. He jumped in and passed his coat back to the boy's mother to wrap around him. The woman looked familiar to Frankie, but he couldn't place her. 'Right, where do you live?' asked

Frankie.

'Number one, New Square. It's just off Bartholomew Street near the cattle market.'

'I know it,' said Frankie. 'We'll be there in five minutes.'

The car sped off and within a few minutes Frankie pulled up outside the alley that led to New Square. He climbed out and opened the back door for the two of them to step out. 'There you are, safe and sound,' said Frankie as he got back into the driver's seat.

'Oh no, you can't go,' said the woman. 'I insist you come in and dry yourself before going anywhere.'

'Thank you,' said Frankie, getting back out and putting on his coat.

The three of them walked up the alley to the front door and the woman opened it and took the boy inside. Frankie followed and shut the door behind him.

'Go into the lounge and make yourself comfortable. I will run a bath and put Bobby in and be back in a moment.'

'Would you like me to make a fire up for you while you are doing that?' asked Frankie.

'Well, if you wouldn't mind,' said the woman gratefully.

Frankie found some papers and screwed them up and placed them in the fire grate. 'Where's the wood?', shouted Frankie up the stairs.

'Outside the back door. There are some logs and an axe,'

replied the woman from the bathroom.

Frankie walked through the kitchen and out the back door. There was a pile of logs but no kindling wood, so Frankie picked up the axe and some dry logs and began splitting some for the fire. He chopped up enough to start the fire and extra for the woman's next one. Then he placed them on the hearth. He added some of the kindling wood and lit the paper. In a few minutes, the kindling wood was burning nicely, so Frankie added two logs and put the guard back around the fireplace.

The woman came back into the room with a large warm towel and handed it to Frankie.

'There we are, Mr Mills. Take this towel upstairs and go in the room on the left. You can get out of your wet things and dry yourself. I have laid out some of my late husband's clothes for you to put on, you look about the same size so hopefully they will fit.'

'Oh, thanks,' said Frankie. 'That's very kind of you.'

'It's the least I can do,' said the woman, 'and please call me Shirley.'

'Okay,' said Frankie, 'and you must call me Frankie'.

The woman returned to Bobby in the bathroom, while Frankie took off his wet clothes and tried on the dry ones. Once dressed, he walked back down the stairs to the fire with his wet clothes in his hand. Shirley walked into the room with Bobby dressed in his dry clothes and took Frankie's wet ones and hung them over the back of a chair near the fire to dry.

'I'll put the kettle on,' said Shirley, disappearing into the kitchen.

Bobby came over to Frankie and sat down next to him, rubbing his hands together, imitating Frankie.

'When you get older,' said Frankie, 'you must learn how to swim, and then you will always be safe in the water.' The boy smiled and replied that he would like to be able to swim like Frankie.

Shirley came back into the room and placed a tray on the table. She poured Bobby a cup of tea in his little cup and then poured Frankie one and passed it to him.

'Thank you,' said Frankie gratefully before taking a mouthful. 'I needed that.'

Shirley turned to Frankie and said how well the clothes fitted him, Frankie thanked her again and smiled.

Shirley smiled back and said, 'I don't believe we've been properly introduced.'

'Well, as you will have heard at the river, my name's Frankie.'

'And mine is Shirley,' said the woman.

'And I'm Bobby,' said the boy, giggling.

'Lovely fire,' said Shirley.

'Thanks,' said Frankie, drinking some more of his tea.

'Did I hear someone say you were a jockey?' asked Shirley.

'Yes,' replied Frankie, 'but I'm retired now.'

'You might have known my late husband,' she said. 'His name was Bob Greenough and he was a jockey too.'

Frankie's blood ran cold, his heart thumping in his chest, guilt welled up as cold and dangerous as the waters of the river. *My God*, thought Frankie, *that's where I know her from.*

Frankie took a deep breath. 'Yes, of course, I did know Bob. I'm so very sorry for your loss, Shirley. He was a very good jockey. A good man.'

Shirley's smile fell for a moment, her gaze darting towards the ground. 'Thank you.'

'I'm hungry,' said Bobby, rubbing his stomach. 'Mum, I'm starving.'

'So am I,' said Frankie, rubbing his stomach too in mimicry of the boy.

Shirley laughed at the two of them, the sadness of the spell suddenly broken. 'I know,' she said, 'why don't we have fish and chips from the chippie up the road?'

'Yippee,' said Bobby. 'I love chips.'

'I'll go up in the car and get us some,' said Frankie.

'Can I come too, please?' asked Bobby.

'Okay, Bobby,' said Frankie. 'Put your shoes on and we will go and get some dinner.'

Shirley said she would put out the plates and cutlery while they were gone.

Frankie and Bobby walked out to the car and got in. Bobby sat in the front passenger seat and Frankie started the car and off they went. Frankie glanced at the eager little face and he could see Bob in him, in the curve of his chin, the shape of his nose. He could feel the guilt there again. It had been abstract before, Bob dying and leaving a wife and son. But it was no longer the grieving doll he had seen at the funeral. No, it was this real, flesh and blood, little boy who had lost his father, and it was all Frankie's fault. He knew he had to do something to help.

The chip shop was only five minutes away. Frankie parked the car outside and the two of them walked in and ordered three fish and chip meals. When they arrived back at the house, Shirley had laid out the plates on the table with knives and forks, along with salt, pepper, tomato sauce and vinegar. Frankie handed her the wrapped food and she put it out on the plates. The three of them started their meal and Shirley chopped up Bobby's fish to make sure there were no bones in it and then buttered a slice of bread each. After dinner, Shirley took Bobby upstairs for his afternoon nap and Frankie said goodbye to the boy.

'Umm... Shirley,' said Frankie hesitantly, 'my wife, Mary, passed away recently and I wondered if you would care to look through her things to see if you would like anything before I take it all to the charity shop? If that's not being too impertinent?'

'Oh, I didn't know,' said Shirley, placing a hand against Frankie's arm. 'I'm so sorry to hear that. It's very kind of you.

And if you ever need to talk about it, well, you know I'm in the same situation.'

'Thank you,' said Frankie, he could feel the grief filling him again. 'Leave it with me and I will sort her things and bring them over one day.'

'We will look forward to seeing you again,' said Shirley happily. She walked over to the fire and felt the clothes on the chair. 'They're all dry and lovely and warm to put on,' she said, handing them to Frankie. He took the clothes from her and walked back upstairs and changed back into them. He left the other clothes on the bed and returned to Shirley in the lounge.

'I've left the others on the bed,' said Frankie. 'Now, I really must go, but I will return again soon.'

Shirley walked Frankie to the door and kissed him on the cheek. 'Thank you so much for saving Bobby, I will forever be in your debt.' Blushing, Frankie waved goodbye as he walked off and Shirley closed the door.

***

Frankie arrived back at the manor and went straight up to the bathroom and ran a bath. He laid back, enjoying a nice soak, thinking about the past few hours and everything that had happened. After a while, Frankie climbed out of the bath, dried himself and put on clean clothes from the wardrobe. He took the ones he had taken off down the stairs to be washed.

That evening, Frankie phoned Stephen and asked if Angela wanted any of Mary's things. Stephen told Frankie that the only thing she would like to remember Mary by was her lovely gold cross and chain.

'Okay,' said Frankie, 'I will bring it with me on Christmas Day. Talking of Christmas, Stephen, I will need your help.'

'Oh, what can I do for you then, Frankie?' asked Stephen.

'Well, I expect Angela has told you I've bought the boys pedal cars and Clare a pram and doll. I've also got your present and there isn't enough room in your car for all of it. So I was wondering if you could take the boy's cars in your vehicle and I will bring the pram and your present in mine.'

'Yes, that's fine. I'll see you Christmas morning then, Frankie.'

'Thanks, Stephen, see you then.'

Frankie walked upstairs and into the spare room. Seeing Mary's possessions again was too much and Frankie sat for a while on the bed, overcome. After a few minutes, Frankie took a deep breath and then he picked up all of Mary's belongings and carefully packed them into her suitcases. Frankie carried them carefully down the stairs and left them by the door.

He stood back and looked at the sad little collection, the things that had once been his wife's and were now as homeless as he felt without her. But Mary had always been generous, had always helped those in need. She would not have wanted Frankie to hoard them when they could be used. *I will return to Shirley's tomorrow with Mary's things and she can choose what she wants.* He picked up Mary's gold cross and chain and put it in a little box Mary had in her drawer, which he then slipped into his suit pocket so he wouldn't forget it on Christmas Day.

Frankie had already made up a fire earlier that morning to be lit on his return from shopping. He picked up the matches from the mantelpiece and lit the fire, and then turned on the radio and sat down in his chair. *If I go to Shirley's tomorrow it will have to be after the radiograms have been delivered*, he thought.

Like a lightbulb turning off, his thoughts drifted from light back to the darkness of the blackmailer, back to the monster that was Ernie. *How can I get rid of him and the letter? Providing, of course, he has actually written a letter. Perhaps it's just a threat.* Frankie doubted Ernie would have written a letter; in fact, Frankie wasn't sure the monster was literate at all.

Suddenly, the fire spluttered and cracked, startling Frankie. Memories, long suppressed, returned. Blackened bodies, the stink of a burned-out farmhouse, echoes of rage and fury and of helplessness to prove what Ernie had done back then. Well, this time Frankie was not helpless. No, this time he would do the right thing and rid the world of Ernie Keep. He would do it the way Ernie would have done, setting fire to the cottage in the middle of the night. It would take care of the blackmailer and the letter, if indeed there was one. But first, he needed to find out if Ernie lived alone. So Frankie decided that, at six a.m. the following morning, he would go to the blackmailer's cottage and watch him leave for work, and then knock at the door to see if anyone else was in the house.

Later that night, Frankie walked up the stairs and into the bathroom. He washed and went into the bedroom, where he undressed and climbed into bed. He set his alarm for six a.m. and laid back on his pillow and closed his eyes.

***

It only seemed like five minutes had passed when the alarm started ringing, a metallic siren. Frankie jumped out of bed and walked to the bathroom. He washed and shaved and then dressed in his dark clothing. He rushed downstairs and into the kitchen and made himself a quick cup of tea, drank it down and walked out the front door and got into his car.

Twenty minutes later, Frankie arrived at the frosty trackway to the cottage. The tall hedges were black against the navy blue of the winter's sky. He drove past and parked down the road, as he did before. He quickly walked back to the track and climbed the bank that ran alongside and into the wood. He slowly made his way through the trees until the cottage came into view. Ernie's car was still parked outside, so Frankie knew he was still at home. It started to rain again, fat, thick droplets, so Frankie found a large tree to take shelter under whilst still being able to see the door to the cottage. He crouched down, pulled his collar up and waited for Ernie to leave.

He had been there a while, shivering and damp, but warmed

by the heat of his own anger. After a while he checked his watch, six-fifty-five. He thought Ernie must be up by now if he was going to leave for work. A few minutes later, Frankie could see a glow coming from inside. *Here he is*, thought Frankie, *he must be getting ready to leave*. It was still dark when the glow in the cottage went out. Frankie hid behind the trunk of the tree and watched, his heart pounding in his chest. Suddenly, the door opened and a large figure appeared in the doorway. A man walked out into the rain, opened the car door and climbed in. Frankie recognised the familiar walk, the defensive stoop. It was definitely Ernie. The headlights came on and Frankie heard the engine start. The car slowly pulled away from the house and disappeared along the muddy track.

Frankie sat and waited, the rain eased and he decided it was time to knock on the door. He had seen a sign up at the entrance to the wood saying it was for sale, so Frankie thought he would use this as an excuse for calling at the cottage. Frankie climbed down the bank and nervously walked up to the door. He knocked hard twice and waited for an answer, but none came. He quickly walked around the cottage, peering in the windows as he went. The cottage looked empty, but Frankie decided to knock once more in case someone was still asleep. He went back to the front door and knocked as loud as he could. Still, there was no answer.

Looks like he lives alone, Frankie thought.

Chapter Eleven

Ypres, Belgium, 1917

The letter was short, the handwriting shaky and untidy, so different from Mary's normal neat and precise script. There was no scent or perfume, no feeling of soul or love or person like the others. It wasn't a letter, it was a quiet, controlled cry of pain. The words themselves were careful, impersonal lest they chink the mental walls Mary must have constructed to contain the grief. Frankie could feel the hurt of the words between the lines and his heart went out in echo of the pain.

> *I regret to inform you that last Saturday my father died...*

How could she forgive Frankie for letting her go through this on her own? First Alfie, now her father; poor Mary was all alone, grieving without Frankie there to look after her.

'She has Angela with her,' said Stephen, as if reading Frankie's mind. He sat down on the filthy firing step, next to his friend. Somewhere in the distance, shells were being exchanged with loud booms and crumps. 'She knows you'd be there if you could.'

'I should be with her, Stephen,' said Frankie, staring down at the hateful little sheet of paper. 'I should be there for her. I should never have signed up for this.'

'We're here to protect her,' replied Stephen. 'To protect them all. Mary understands, her father would have understood. You've done everything you can to look after her, and when the war is over you'll be there for her.'

'I hate this war,' snapped Frankie. 'I hate this place, I hate the trenches, I hate it.'

'We all do,' said Stephen gently. 'I wish I could go home too, to spend time with Angela, to see if there is something there. We'll get there, eventually. We're winning, you know that. It'll all be over soon. But right now, you must write back to Mary, let her know you're thinking of her.'

'It's changed me, you know.' Frankie gestured around the dank, damp trench. 'All this. I'm not the same person I was before... before we came out here. I feel numb all the time. Or angry or scared. What if I do make it home and Mary doesn't like this new me?'

'It's changed us all, Frankie. War does that. But you're still you. When we get back, we can forget all about this and be ourselves again. Now go write to Mary, tell her you love her and you'll be home one day and it'll all be all right. Mary will be your anchor; she will see you safe. Frankie, it'll be all right, I promise.'

Speen Moor Manor, Newbury, 1936

It was getting light outside Frankie's window, so he got up and went out the back door to the stable. He opened the doors and Jennet walked over to him.

'Hello, old girl,' said Frankie, pouring some water into Jennet's trough. 'It's bit wet out here today so you'd better stay here in the warm.' He looked her over to make sure she was all right and closed up the doors and bolted them shut.

Now, where shall I put the radiogram when it arrives, thought Frankie. He looked around the room and decided that if he moved Mary's table with her knitting box on, he could then have the radiogram there. He had forgotten all about Mary's knitting box when he had packed her things away so he picked it up and put it with the suitcases, ready to take to Shirley. *Maybe she might use it*, he thought.

Frankie thought about little Bobby and decided he would call the store in Reading and get them to send another blue pedal car, gift wrapped, for Bobby. *I think I'll also buy Shirley an expensive bottle of perfume and have it gift wrapped*. He got up and walked to the front door, opened it and carried the suitcases and Mary's knitting box to the car and laid them on the back seat and then locked the door. Frankie walked back up the steps and into the study. The fire was dying down so he put on another log and sat back down in his chair.

Nearly lunch time and still no sign of the radiograms being delivered, Frankie thought. He got up and walked into the kitchen and looked in the cupboards to see what he could have for dinner. *Almost out of supplies*, thought Frankie. He spotted a tin of Irish stew in the back of the cupboard and decided it would have to do. He made a mental note that he needed to buy more groceries when he went out.

He picked up a small saucepan from the cupboard and emptied the contents of the tin into it. He placed the saucepan on a low heat on the stove. While that was being cooked, Frankie cut two slices of bread, buttered them and placed them on the side of a large plate. He took a spoon and started stirring the stew. After a few minutes, it started to bubble so Frankie poured it out onto his plate and put the empty saucepan in the sink. He picked up his spoon and began to eat. *Not bad*, he thought after taking a mouthful.

He finished his dinner and put the plate into the sink with the saucepan. He wandered back into the study and sat down in his chair. *Perhaps they won't come until tomorrow*, he thought. Frankie slowly started to nod off, when a loud knock at the door woke him up. He quickly walked to the front door and opened it. A man in a brown overall stood at the bottom of the steps, 'Mr Mills?' he asked.

'Yes,' said Frankie.

'We have two radiograms to be delivered to you.'

'Yes, bring them in, please,' said Frankie.

There was another man in the back of the lorry who helped carry the radiograms into the house. The first one was gift wrapped, as Frankie had asked, and was put to one side in the entrance. The other was carried into the study and put into the place where Frankie had decided to have it.

'There we are, sir. All done.'

Frankie put some money into one of the men's hand and thanked them as he closed the door. He plugged in the radiogram and read through the instructions. He then turned the knob along to his local channel and on came the music, loud and clear. *How wonderful*, thought Frankie, *Stephen and Angela are going to love theirs*. He turned it off. *Plenty of time for that later.*

Frankie put on his shoes and walked into the hall, took his hat and coat down from the peg and put them on. He opened the front door and went down the steps to the car. He got in and drove slowly into town. Frankie pulled up outside the shop where he used to buy Mary's perfume, locked his door and walked in.

'Hello,' said the lady behind the counter.

'Hello,' replied Frankie, 'I'm looking for a bottle of the Blue Lagoon perfume.'

'Standard or large, sir?'

'I'd like the large size, please,' said Frankie.

The lady reached into the glass case and came out with a beautiful bottle with a blue-glass lady on the top. 'Would you like it gift wrapped, sir?'

'Yes, please,' said Frankie. 'It's a Christmas gift for a friend.'

'A very lucky lady,' said the woman behind the counter. 'This is one of our most expensive perfumes.'

Frankie paid the woman and said goodbye.

Back in the car, Frankie drove along the road to Shirley's at New Square. He pulled up outside the entrance to the alley and parked the car. He got out the two suitcases and began walking along the alley to Shirley's house. As he approached, Bobby came running out of the front door.

'Hello, Bobby,' said Frankie, smiling. The boy grinned back excitedly and Frankie felt a happiness at the sight.

Shirley came walking out and greeted Frankie with a 'nice to see you again'.

Frankie said, 'I've brought the things I told you about,' and he handed the two suitcases to Shirley. 'I've just got to go back to the car and fetch the rest.'

Frankie turned and walked back to the car, closely followed by Bobby. He picked up the sewing box from the back seat and put it down on the path while he locked the car. He picked it up and carried it back to Shirley's with Bobby close behind. He handed Shirley the box and said, 'I don't know if you knit, Shirley, but this was Mary's knitting box.'

'Oh, yes,' said Shirley, 'I do and I'm sure I will use it, thank you. Could you bring the suitcases upstairs and then I'll empty them and give you them back.'

'You can keep the cases as well,' said Frankie. 'They were Mary's and I have my own.'

'Oh, thank you very much,' said Shirley. 'I'm sure they will come in handy when Bobby and I go on holiday in the summer.'

'Anything you don't want,' said Frankie, 'you can give to charity or do with what you like. Honestly, you're doing me a favour. I don't think I could do it myself, getting rid of Mary's things to charity.'

'Thank you,' said Shirley, walking back down the stairs. 'Have you got time for a cup of tea?'

'Of course,' said Frankie, smiling.

'Father Christmas is coming soon,' said Bobby, jumping up and down all excited.

'Yes, he is,' said Frankie, 'and I believe he is bringing you an extra special present for being such a good boy.'

'Yippee!' shouted Bobby.

'Oh, you haven't?' hissed Shirley with a bewildered smile.

'Well, it's just a little thing,' said Frankie, 'and the boy's had a rough few weeks. Besides, my Mary would have bought him something. We never had children of our own and she loved the chance to buy for them. I do too.'

'Well, that's very kind of you,' said Shirley gratefully. 'You've been so kind.'

Frankie smiled and drank his tea, although he felt a spike of guilt for the small family.

'By the way, what are you and Bobby doing at Christmas?'

'Nothing special,' said Shirley, 'we'll be celebrating here as usual. Why do you ask?'

'Well, I'm going to my friends for Christmas dinner and will be home around tea time. I was wondering, if it wouldn't be too presumptuous, if I could call by with Bobby's present then? If that's all right?'

'We would love to see you on Christmas Day,' said Shirley happily.

'Okay,' said Frankie.

'We'll look forward to seeing you then,' said Shirley, smiling.

Frankie got up and walked to the door, followed by Shirley. 'Where's Bobby? I'd like to say goodbye before I go.'

Shirley shouted to Bobby who was playing in the back garden, 'Bobby, Frankie's going.'

Bobby came running through the house and out of the front door. 'Goodbye, Frankie,' he said.

Shirley and Frankie laughed at the little boy's remark. 'Goodbye,' said Frankie and he waved to Shirley and Bobby as he drove away.

***

Back in town, Frankie pulled over at the grocery store and walked in. He tried to think of everything he had run out of and chucked in a few extras as he went. He put the two heavy bags of shopping in the back of the car and shut the door. Frankie arrived home, got out of the car, unlocked the front door of the house and opened it wide. He returned to the car and picked up the two heavy bags of shopping and Shirley's box with the perfume in and then carried it all inside.

Frankie unpacked the groceries in the kitchen and put them all away. He cut himself a nice slice of walnut cake and put it on a small plate and walked into the study. He quickly made up a fire and turned on his new radiogram. He poured himself a whisky and sat down in his chair and listened to the music.

A while later, the phone rang and Frankie picked it up. 'Frankie Mills speaking,' he said.

'Hello, Mr Mills, it's Inspector George Allen here. I'm just phoning to let you know a date has now been set for the pre-trial of the man arrested for your wife's murder. It's the 29th at ten-thirty in the Number One Court at the assizes in Reading. The judge will be deciding whether to proceed to full trial.'

My God, thought Frankie, trying hard not to think of the innocent man currently taking the blame for his actions. His whole body shaking, Frankie took a deep breath, before he replied. 'That's very quick. Thank you for letting me know, Inspector.'

'You'll not be required to give evidence, but we hope you can attend. I'm sure you would like to see justice done.'

Frankie said he would be there and thanked the inspector again before putting the phone down.

I need longer, I need more time. But there is no more time. I will deal with Ernie tonight.

Frankie got up and looked out of the window. Outside the sky was bright and crisp and it had been dry all day. With any luck the thatch on the Ernie's cottage would have dried out enough to catch alight. The forecast for the rest of the night was dry too, so Frankie decided to go ahead with his plan and burn the cottage to the ground, with Ernie asleep inside. He deserved it, for all he had done. It would be a fitting punishment for an evil man.

Still shaking from the inspector's call, Frankie went out to the shed and picked up the can of petrol he kept there and took it inside the house. He decided he would take a short length of hose and a funnel so he might put the hose quietly through the letterbox, add the funnel to the end and then pour the petrol down through it. He took all three items out to the car and put them in the boot.

It was time for Frankie to take revenge on Ernie.

Chapter Twelve

Ypres, Belgium, 1917

The sudden rattle of the machine gun was the sound of death. Three men were torn apart in a cloud of blood, flesh and bone before Frankie even realised he had already thrown himself to the ground. Another two men, both inexperienced new recruits were killed after, too slow, still allowing their brains to think before their bodies reacted; a third man was hit in the belly and now screamed in awful agony as the last minutes of his life slipped away. Six seconds, six lives.

The company was pinned down now. The deadly gunfire gone off to take other lives for now, but a hint of movement, a carelessly raised head and then death would be back to reap another harvest.

Lieutenant Bradley-Smythe had been marked up as yet another useless Rupert when he'd first been assigned to the company. Another talentless private school boy brought up on Ivanhoe and Arthur and misty-eyed notions of death or glory, notions that would get the company killed in pursuit of a mention in dispatches. Smithy, as they'd nicknamed him, had proven different. Thoughtful, clever and unwilling to waste lives, the now grizzled veterans had grown to trust this young warrior, to respect and even to like him. That he'd be prepared for this situation, that he'd thought to bring a periscope with him to look over the edge of the shell-crater shelter, was no surprise.

'The Bosch nest is in those trees, twenty-five, thirty yards to the west,' Smithy said, still lying prone. He reached awkwardly into his waist pouch and withdrew a pair of grenades. 'I need a pair of volunteers to crawl back around and take it out for us. Knock out that nest and the rest of us can leg it to the trees.'

'I'll go, sir,' said Frankie. He was throbbing with rage and he wanted to kill, to get revenge for his lost friends. He accepted the grenades and placed them into his pouch.

'Good man! Mills bombs for Mills!' bellowed Smithy. 'Who else?'

'I'll go, sir,' volunteered Stephen.

'No, I need you here, Sergeant. What about you, Keep?'

'Me, sir?' Ernie looked horrified. 'But... I...'

'Good man. Follow Mills, he's ranking here.'

Frankie saluted, pulled his rifle onto his back and slithered to the crater's edge, furthest from the machine-gun fire. Staying on his belly, he kicked himself up and into no man's land. The ground was a butcher's yard, bodies and parts of bodies littered the area, although most were from the previous day's failed assault. Artillery shells and bullets rained overhead, stalling the attack. Frankie knew if he failed today, his company would be trapped until darkness fell and, even then, they faced a deadly journey back to their trenches. If he failed, more of his friends would die.

Taking a deep breath, Frankie leopard crawled in a wide arc for about two-hundred yards, ignoring the horrors, and dropped into a deep crater a short dash from the woodland. Seconds later, Ernie dropped in behind him. Carefully, Frankie peeped over the edge of the crater. He could see the machine-gun nest well from here. He could clearly make out the brutal MG08 and even make out the dirt-covered faces of the four-man crew. He was still too far for the grenades, however. For a second, Frankie considered trying to shoot them. He was confident he could take one or even two of the team but, if he failed, the gun would swing in his direction and that would be that. No, he needed a more close-up method of attack.

'Okay,' he said, turning to Ernie. 'On the count of three, we rush the woods. I'll get a bomb on them and we follow up with rifle and bayonet, yes?'

Ernie spat on to the ground and pulled a ration-issue cigarette from a pocket. 'No fear,' he said, pulling out a box of matches. 'I'm not getting myself killed for some snooty kid. We stay here to nightfall, then we go home. Say we tried, but couldn't get close.'

'We have orders!' snapped Frankie. 'Men will die if we don't do it.'

'Well, you go then,' replied Ernie, lighting his cigarette. 'You ain't getting me over there.'

'You're a coward, Ernie Keep.'

Ernie laughed. 'I'm a living one.'

Frankie turned away in fury. He glanced up again. The Germans were firing far to his left, slaughtering a group of men who were trying to get to cover. Fighting back his fear, Frankie threw himself up and over, his head down as he ran full pelt towards the wood.

Those ten seconds or so were the most terrifying of Frankie's life so far. With every gasped and choked breath, he expected to be cut down by red hot lead. However, it took the Germans a few seconds to spot him, to relay the message and to swing the gun around. Frankie felt a hammer-like thud on his helmet and the puff of bullets as he dived into cover. He hit the ground hard, agony sweeping through him.

Frankie scrambled to the cover of a blasted tree stump, heart pounding. He checked himself over in terror, expecting to finding a fatal wound. The pain came from a flesh wound in his upper-left arm. The bullet having torn through his skin and muscle, but passing out without touching bone. Bleeding and painful, but not enough to stop him provided he moved quickly. His helmet too had been a close call, another bullet scraping the edge of the steel but not penetrating.

Frankie gritted his teeth. Holding his rifle in one hand and a Mills bomb in the other, he crawled his way through the woodland towards the nest. He could feel the deafening rattle now, only a few feet away.

'*Tommys da drüben. Beim Krater,*' roared a voice.

Frankie attacked. Pulling the pin from the grenade, he threw it at the gun itself, swinging up his rifle as the bomb exploded in a shower of earth, stones and fire. Before the dust had settled, Frankie was charging. Two of the crew were already down and Frankie quickly put four rounds into the third. The fourth German was fast, drawing his Luger he snapped off a shaky shot that missed Frankie by less than an inch, but Frankie had momentum now and barrelled into the man, knocking him over. Cold agony tore up his shoulder, but Frankie's rage overwhelmed the pain as he smashed the butt of his Lee-Enfield into the man's face, over and over.

***

Spleen Moor Manor, Newbury, 1936

At three a.m., the alarm sounded and Frankie reached over and turned it off. The truth was he had barely slept, his mind rolling over the plan, again and again and again. Thankful it was finally time to take action, he got up out of bed and walked into the bathroom. He washed and then dressed in his dark clothes and walked down the stairs. He pulled a black pair of gloves from the drawer and put them in his coat pocket. He then went into the kitchen, made a strong cup of tea and sat thinking again about the next couple of hours and what had to be done.

He finished his drink, took off his slippers and put on his shoes. He reached up and took down his hat and coat from its peg and put them on. Suddenly, he paused and then returned to the kitchen to retrieve a rag and bottle of paraffin oil from the cupboard under the sink. Frankie quietly opened the front door and looked out. Everywhere was quiet. Frankie walked down the steps, unlocked the car door and got in. He quietly pulled the car door shut and started the engine, pulled away from the house and drove off to Ernie's cottage at Penn Wood.

When Frankie arrived at the trackway leading to the cottage, he reversed down the track until his car was hidden from the main road. He sat there for a few minutes longer, his courage wavering in and out. Frankie had faced these moments before, in the war, with an enemy who would have killed him on sight, but this, to kill a sleeping man in cold blood, this was a different prospect entirely. Ernie deserved it; Frankie knew. If not for the blackmail and for causing Mary's death, then for all the crimes he had committed during the war – murder, robbery, cowardice. Had Frankie been able to have proven it then, Ernie would have been shot and perhaps lives could have been saved. Frankie had failed to stop Ernie back then and it had cost him everything he cared about. He couldn't fail again. Tonight, he was justice herself.

Heart pounding, Frankie stepped out into the cold of the winter's morning. There was some moonlight to see by, but otherwise the dark was inky and infinite; still, Frankie knew where he was going. He took out the can of petrol, the hose and the funnel and closed the boot quietly. He put on his gloves, picked up the three items and slowly walked the remaining one-hundred-and-sixty yards to the cottage.

The solitary building stood black against the deep blue of the darkness. Aware of the crunch of his feet on the frozen gravel, Frankie walked carefully up to the front door and put everything on the ground. His whole body shaking, he tried to glimpse through the darkened windows, but could see nothing, and decided he had to trust that Ernie was alone.

Frankie gently pushed open the letterbox, the hinges squeaking quietly as they were forced back, then he picked up the length of hose and slowly passed it through the

147

letterbox until only a foot or so remained outside. His hands shaking, he picked up the funnel and put it in the end of the hose. He then picked up the can and began slowly pouring the petrol, two handed, into the funnel and down the hose into the cottage. He could smell the fumes, wafting out, strong and acrid, and wondered if they might wake the sleeping Ernie, but it was too late now, too late to go back.

After emptying about half the can, Frankie carefully placed it back on the ground before removing the funnel and quietly pulling the hose back out. Frankie left the hose and funnel on the ground and walked around the cottage, spilling petrol over the wooden windows as he went. There was no back door, so Frankie used the remainder of the petrol on the thatch, splashing it up onto the moss-covered reeds as far as he could reach. When all the petrol had been used, Frankie picked up the can and hose in one hand and the funnel in the other and walked back to the car. He opened the boot, retrieved the rag and paraffin oil and put all the other items inside. He then opened the car door and put the key in the ignition, ready for a quick getaway.

He walked back to the cottage with his heart pounding in his ears. Unscrewing the bottle, he doused the rag in the oil and stuffed it through the letterbox so that half of the cloth was still outside. His hands shaking, he took the matches from his pocket and lit them two together. It took three attempts, but he finally lit the rag and retreated back to the entrance to the garden. Frankie watched as the flame raced up the old cloth and in through the letterbox. There was a sudden loud whooshing noise and the whole inside of the small house lit up.

Frankie didn't want to stop to watch. If Ernie started

screaming, Frankie wasn't sure he wouldn't try to help. Dragging himself away, he ran back along the track, careless of the noise, and jumped into the car. He started the engine and drove quickly along the track and out onto the main road. He made sure there was no traffic coming from either direction and headed back towards his house.

As he pulled up outside his house and turned off the engine, Frankie could hear the distant sounds of fire engines. He waited for a moment to make sure no one had heard him pull up and then got out of the car and walked up the steps to the door. Once inside, he took off all his clothes and put them in the washer. He quickly ran up the stairs and put on his dressing gown, scrubbing his hands with perfumed soap to get rid of the paraffin smell.

Back downstairs, he walked into the study and poured himself a large glass of whisky, drank it back and poured another. Frankie sat in his chair, thinking about the items in the boot. *They'll be all right there for the rest of the night*, he thought. He closed his eyes and saw again the whoosh of flame, the glow of the house. It was over, justice at last for all of those Ernie had hurt. Justice for Mary. He drank the rest of the drink and slowly walked up the stairs to bed.

Chapter Thirteen

Ypres, Belgium, 1917

Dear Frankie,

I hope you are well?

I wanted to send a quick note to say just how proud of you we all are, showing the Bosch what for. Congratulations on your medal. You made the local paper; I attach a copy.

Mary is doing well, despite her father and all that. She talks about you a lot, and everyone sends their best wishes to you and Stephen.

The horses...

Frankie placed the letter down next to him and unfolded the small square of newspaper that had been tucked inside. *Local Man Awarded Military Medal for Gallantry.* Gallantry? Frankie sneered at the word. He had killed four men that day and that did not feel particularly gallant. He had killed four sons, four husbands, fathers, brothers, uncles. Had he made widows? Had he made orphans of their children? Frankie didn't know who they had been before the war. Had they been good men or bad? Had they been any different from him or Stephen, or even poor Archie?

How can it have been a gallant thing? Yes, they had killed too, they had been killing many more. They would have killed his whole company if they needed to, and he had done what he did because it needed to be done. He did not regret the killing, no more than he regretted the other lives he had taken, but to be feted for it, to be called gallant. Frankie screwed up the little square of paper and threw it into the mud. He was a killer because he had to be, and he accepted that, but he didn't have to accept being called a hero.

***

Spleen Moor Manor, Newbury, 1936

The clock showed the time to be seven-fifty a.m. when Frankie opened his bleary eyes. He could still smell petrol and paraffin on his skin, so he ran himself a bath. While the bath was filling, Frankie laid out some clean clothes on the bed. He turned off the taps and slowly lowered himself into the scalding water. He washed himself and then laid back, his mind drifting back to the cottage and what he had done. *Hopefully that will be the end of it all, with Ernie gone and the letter destroyed,* he thought. *The homeless man will be found not guilty, I'm sure, and if not then I will confess. I did the right thing, I know it.*

After a good soaking, he climbed out of the bath, applied rather too much aftershave to cover any lingering smell, and put on his dressing gown. He put his feet into his slippers and walked down the stairs and into the kitchen. He filled the kettle with water and, while it was boiling, Frankie walked into the study and made up a fire. He turned on his radiogram for the news and went back into the kitchen to make a cup of tea. He took his cup back into the study and sat down in his chair by the fire.

Christmas carols were playing on the radiogram and Frankie realised it was Christmas Eve. *Well, tomorrow's the big day*, he thought to himself. *Mary loved Christmas, I'm not sure I could have faced it alone*. He was looking forward to Christmas dinner with the Sheehans and giving everyone their presents. But was equally as excited at going to Shirley and Bobby's later in the day. He knew Mary would have wanted him to treat the boy. It seemed right to have spent her money on him.

He listened to the news at eight-thirty a.m., but nothing was mentioned about the fire. He picked up his cup and took it into kitchen and placed it in the sink. He slowly walked back up the stairs to his bedroom and dressed. It felt good to be dressed in clean clothes and the smell of petrol had now gone.

Frankie went back down the stairs and walked out the back door to the shed. He picked up an old sack and took it with him to the car parked out front. He opened the boot, took out the hose and funnel he had used and put them in the sack. He then lifted out the empty petrol can and carried it all back inside the house.

Frankie took the empty petrol can and put it in the shed, locked the door and then put the sack with its contents in the dustbin. Frankie opened the stable doors and led Jennet out along the path to the paddock. He opened the gate and let her run free. Frankie stood watching her for a moment and then turned and walked back to the stable. He spent about an hour cleaning out and then put down clean bedding before closing the doors. Frankie decided that as it was a lovely crisp day, he would leave Jennet out in the paddock until he returned from town.

Back in the house, Frankie washed his hands and put on his hat and coat, before walking out the door and getting into the car. As he drove down the road to the café by the river, he thought about the last time he had come to have his lunch there and ended up saving little Bobby's life. *Please can today be less eventful.*

Entering the café, Frankie was directed to a table by the window. The waitress came over to the table and asked if he wanted to order.

'Hello,' said Frankie, 'I would like a pot of tea and my usual, the shepherd's pie, please.'

The girl looked up from her pad in surprise, 'Oh, sorry, Mr Mills, I didn't realise it was you. Please hold on a minute.'

Frankie sat nervously as the girl turned and walked back to the kitchen. Moments later, she returned with the cook, a beefy-looking man dressed in pristine chef's whites. As he came over, he held out one ham-like hand, crushing Frankie's own in a fiercely vigorous handshake.

'Mr Mills, it's an honour to have you as a patron. I would like you to accept this meal as a "thank you" from the whole community, for saving that little boy in the river. Whatever you'd like, it's on the house,' said the cook.

Frankie thanked him, a little taken back. 'News travels fast, doesn't it?'

The cook replied, 'It does when it's all over the front page of the *Newbury News.*'

The girl came forward and passed the paper to Frankie. There was a picture of Frankie with Bobby, who had his arm around Frankie's neck. And behind the two of them stood Shirley, looking relieved and shocked in equal measure. Scanning the article, Frankie saw the story told of how the boy fell into the river and how Frankie had saved him and then brought the boy back to life.

'They're exaggerating a little bit. I only did what anyone would have done in the same circumstances,' said Frankie.

'I don't think so, Mr Mills; you're a hero saving that boy's life and risking your own.' The cook turned to the rest of the people in the café. 'Ladies and gents, please put your hands together for Mr Mills, the man that saved little Bobby Greenough.'

Everyone clapped and cheered and the waitress put Frankie's pot of tea on the table.

'Sorry about that,' said the girl, 'but the cook told me to tell him if you came in.'

'Oh, it's all right,' said Frankie, feeling thankful he had done something good to balance some of the harm of the last few weeks.

The cook arrived with Frankie's dinner. 'And all on the house,' he said as he walked back to the kitchen.

Frankie relaxed and ate his meal quietly and drank his tea. The girl returned and asked if Frankie would like a dessert.

'No, thank you,' said Frankie. 'I'm full after my lovely dinner.'

'Well, if you need anything else…'

A sudden idea popped into Frankie's mind.

'An odd question, maybe, but have you heard if there was a fire somewhere last night? I was woken by the loud bells from a fire engine in the early hours but I've not heard about the cause.'

'I haven't heard anything,' said the girl. 'I'll ask the cook when I go back in the kitchen.'

Frankie poured the last of the tea into his cup and added the milk and sugar. He could see clouds gathering out of the window and thought rain could be on the way and Jennet must be got in.

As he was finishing his tea, the waitress walked up to his table and said, 'You're right about a fire, Mr Mills. The cook told me there were some firemen in for breakfast. They said a man had been saved from a burning cottage just outside of town and was now in a coma in hospital with very severe burns.'

My God, he's still alive. Ernie Keep is still alive. Frankie's heart started pounding again. If Ernie woke up, surely he would point the blame at Frankie. Everything would come out, Mary, Bob and now Ernie, everything.

'Oh dear,' said Frankie stiffly, 'how awful.' He gave the girl a tip and thanked the cook for the lovely free meal.

Frankie drove quickly home and raced straight out to the paddock where Jennet stood waiting by the gate. Frankie opened it and led her back into the stable. He picked up a towel and gave her a good rub down, ensuring she was perfectly dry. Then he gave her a couple of pats down the neck and closed up the doors for the night. *What am I going to do about Ernie? Should I go into the hospital and smother him? Is that too dangerous?* His mind a whirl of emotions.

Frankie walked back into the study and made up a fire. After which, he took off his hat and coat and hung them up on the peg. He returned to the study, took off his shoes and put on his slippers and poured himself a glass of whisky and sat down in his chair. He took a swallow of the drink and thought about the next day, it being Christmas Day.

Suddenly, there was a knock at the door. Frankie put down his glass, got up and went to answer it. Two men stood on the doorstep.

'Mr Mills?' one asked.

'Yes,' said Frankie.

'We have a delivery for you.'

Good God, thought Frankie, *I'd totally forgotten about the delivery of the children's presents.* The two men lifted down three big boxes and carried them into the house. One then returned to the lorry and came back with two smaller boxes. Frankie tipped and thanked them, and then shut the door. He looked at the three large boxes and saw someone had written red on one of the boxes and blue on the other two.

Frankie thought he would go to the graveyard first thing in the morning to visit Mary's grave. Stephen would be arriving late morning and the two of them would take the presents and return to Stephen's house for Christmas dinner. After which he would go to Shirley and Bobby's with their gifts. Which reminded Frankie, he had not put any name tags on the presents. He quickly went up the stairs to the bedroom and lifted down a box with Christmas paper and tags in. He took a handful of tags and returned to the study.

Frankie sat down at the bureau and wrote on one: *To Stephen and Angela, wishing you both a very Merry Christmas, love Frankie*. It felt strange not to write Mary's name too. He took it out into the hallway and stuck it on the big box containing the radiogram. Next, he did two for Clare and stuck them on the boxes containing her pram and doll. And then the boys and stuck the tags on their boxes with the pedal cars in. Then he did the same for Bobby's pedal car and, lastly, wrote one out for Shirley and put it on her box of perfume. *That's it, all done and ready for tomorrow*, he thought and he sat back in his chair.

Chapter Fourteen

Ypres, Belgium, 1917

Dearest Frankie,

*I hope you are safe and well. There is not an
hour that goes by that I do not think about
you and pray for your safe return. Please do
stay safe!*

*Well, I promised I would write and let you
know how our little holiday went. You were
right, of course, it did me the world of good
to get away from sorting out Dad's things
after the funeral. There were so many
people at the funeral, Frankie; it was lovely
to see how many people cared about Dad.*

*Jack from next door came around too and I
said he could put his lambs in the paddock.
When you are home, you will love to see
them gambolling and playing about. One
day, our own little babies will be laughing
and running there too. Hold on to that
thought, Frankie, if you ever feel down –*

one day you and I will be holding hands in our lovely house, watching our babies play!

So, the holiday. Well, as you know, Angela and I went to Charmouth, like you said we should. We stayed in a lovely little B&B just a few minutes from the beach. It was run by a lady called Mrs Fish. Can you believe it? Mrs Fish living by the sea?

We went fossil hunting, just like your dad used to take you. I can just imagine you there on the beach picking amongst the rocks to find new additions for your collection. Well, Angela found a lovely one within a few minutes, one of those ammonite things, like a little curly snail! And then she found one that looked golden, although it is iron apparently and has gone black since we have been home.

We met another fossil hunter who had found a piece of backbone from an ancient reptile, a bit like a dolphin – although it looked like a flattened pebble to me. Anyway, would you believe it, the next day we went to Lyme Regis and I only went and found one of the backbone pieces myself. Such an amazing thing to find something that could be two-hundred million years old.

Angela has sketched out a few of our finds to show you; she is becoming quite the

*artist. Well, it was a lovely little holiday and
I am so pleased you suggested it.*

*I cannot wait for you to come home so I can
show you everything.*

All my love, always,

Mary.

***

Spleen Moor Manor, Newbury, 1936

It was Christmas Day, not that it felt like it. Ever since he'd
returned from France, Christmas had been Mary's day. She
had loved it with a childlike passion. She loved the
traditions, loved buying the gifts, writing the cards and
visiting friends, especially Angela and Stephen who had
shared every one with them for the past seventeen years.
Frankie had barely even thought of cards this year. Of
course, Mary had already sent most of them out before…
well, before, and those she hadn't Frankie couldn't bring
himself to complete. Those he had received had been filled
with condolences, rather than cheer. Frankie knew there
would be gifts for him too, from Mary, secreted away in her
little spot in the attic, and Frankie dreaded the thought he
would have to retrieve them at some point.

For the first time in seventeen years, he had awoken on
Christmas Day at his normal time without Mary singing him
awake early with carols. There was no sweet smell of baking
pies to take to the Sheehans, no gifts, no stolen kisses under

the mistletoe, no mistletoe at all. There was just the drab winter's weather and the fear he might spoil the day for both the Sheehans and Greenoughs. No, Frankie would not do that. Mary would have hated for the children's day to be less than perfect; he would get through this for her.

For breakfast, Frankie poured himself a whisky. He would not normally have dreamed of such a thing, but today he missed Mary with such a fierce and painful longing that he needed something. Frankie opened the back door and walked out to the stable. He opened both doors and said 'Merry Christmas' to Jennet and she responded with a warm nuzzle of his hands. As it was to remain dry for the day, Frankie wanted to leave Jennet out in the paddock, but decided he would get Jennet back in before he went to Shirley's in the afternoon. Frankie opened the gate, gave Jennet a couple of sugar knobs and let her walk away into the field. He watched her run straight across the length of the paddock to the far end, where the horse next door was looking over the fence.

It was time to visit Mary. The time of year meant there were no flowers to be found in the garden; however, Frankie was able to collect up a good amount of holly and mistletoe from the trees at the back of the paddock, which he wrapped together with some strands of ivy. Despite his low mood, he smiled at his handiwork. Mary would have loved the festive bouquet, with the bright reds and whites of the berries taking the place of summer flowers.

Shaw graveyard was remarkably busy with visitors sharing their love with their departed family. Frankie was forced to park some distance away and walk along the narrow path to the graveyard. The place filled Frankie with dread now, memories crowding his mind, regrets too, of course, and when he came to Mary's grave, with its newly installed headstone and wilting flowers, he couldn't help but burst into tears. He stood there for a moment, as if scared to approach, then finally walked over and took out the dying stems from the vase and replaced them with his festive spray.

'Merry Christmas, my love,' he said, running his palm down the smooth cold stone as if he were caressing her face. 'I miss you so much. I'm off to Stephen and Angela's for Christmas dinner. I'm giving Angela your gold cross and chain; I know you would've liked her to have it. Jennet is fine and I've left her out in the paddock for a few hours as it's supposed to be a dry day.

'I miss you, Mary, I cannot wait until we can be together again, and until that time I will do everything I can to atone for all I've done. I love you.' Frankie then said goodbye to Mary and walked slowly back to the car.

***

Back at the house, Frankie checked all the presents were correctly labelled and then felt in his pocket to make sure he had the little box with Mary's cross and chain in. He left the fire to die down and waited for Stephen to arrive. Frankie suddenly realised if Stephen saw his new radiogram and then saw the size of their present, he would probably guess what it was. So Frankie decided not to let Stephen into the study, but to load the presents as soon as he arrives and then set off.

'Merry Christmas, Frankie,' said Stephen as he walked into the hall.

'And Merry Christmas to you, Stephen,' said Frankie, happy to see his friend.

'How are you doing today?' asked Stephen gently. 'It must be hard.'

'Today was always Mary's day,' replied Frankie. 'I'm not sure I will ever get used to it, nor do I want to.'

'Of course, but it will get easier with time. You and I know that better than most,' said Stephen, placing a reassuring hand on Frankie's arm.

Frankie nodded. 'Well, if you take that present there, Stephen, and put it on the back seat of your car. I will bring the others out.'

Stephen carried the big box down the steps to the car and put it down on the ground while he opened the back door. He picked up the box and laid it on the back seat. Frankie told Stephen to push it over as far as it would go so there would be enough room for the other box. 'Just fits,' said Stephen, pushing the second box into place.

Frankie came back out of the house with two slightly smaller packages and asked Stephen to open the boot on Frankie's car so he could put them in.

'Right, now for the biggest and heaviest box,' said Frankie. 'We'll carry it down the steps to my car and then I will open the door the other side and pull it across the seat.'

'Good God, what have you got in here, Frankie? A safe?' said Stephen jokingly.

'This is for you and Angela,' said Frankie smiling.

They lifted the big heavy box in through the car door and onto the edge of the seat.

'Right,' said Frankie, 'let me get it from the other side and you push when I say. Okay, Stephen, push it now.' Frankie pulled the box across the seat and into position. 'That's it, Stephen, all done.'

Frankie closed the front door of the house and then walked back to his car. 'I'll follow you,' said Frankie.

'Okay, Frankie, I'll take it nice and slow.' They both climbed into their cars and set off.

A quarter of an hour later, both cars pulled up outside Stephen's house. Mark and Christopher were playing football and Clare was sat on a blanket on the lawn having a tea party for her dolls. They all came running over as Frankie and Stephen got out of their cars.

'Merry Christmas,' said Frankie.

'Merry Christmas and a Happy New Year,' said the children, all laughing.

Angela came walking out of the house, embraced Frankie and wished him a Merry Christmas.

'And to you, Angela,' replied Frankie.

'I think Frankie's bought us a safe for Christmas,' Stephen

said to Angela, kissing her on the cheek and laughing as he spoke.

'A safe?' replied Angela questioningly.

'Oh, he's joking, Angela,' said Frankie. 'It's just a little heavy.'

'What do you want to do with the presents?' Stephen asked Frankie.

'I think we'll leave them until after dinner, if that's all right with everyone?' said Frankie.

The children were all looking through the car's windows, trying to guess what might be in the big boxes. Frankie locked the doors on his car and followed Stephen and Angela into the house.

'What a beautiful day it is for a Christmas Day,' said Angela, 'so mild for the time of year.'

'Yes,' said Frankie. 'Just the sort of day Mary used to enjoy, a crisp winter day. I put Jennet out in the paddock today as it was so nice. Talking of which, I wondered if Clare would like Jennet?' Frankie then whispered, 'I mean if anything should happen to me. I know it's a bit morbid on Christmas Day but now Mary's gone and there's no one else to leave anything to, I wondered if she might like her?'

'Frankie, come on. Let's not talk of such things,' replied Angela. 'Clare will enjoy coming over to you for a horse ride for years to come.'

'Well here, at least, is the little gift of Mary's I promised you,' said Frankie. He pulled the little box from his pocket and passed it to Angela. She opened it and said how lovely it was. Stephen took the cross and chain from her and hung it around her neck.

'It looks really lovely against your red dress,' said Stephen. Angela thanked Frankie and gave him a kiss on the cheek. She admired herself for a moment in front of the mirror and adjusted her lovely nut-brown hair before going into the kitchen.

The two boys came running in, asking about their presents from Uncle Frankie. Stephen told them they could open them after dinner. The boys ran back into the garden and continued playing their game.

'Would you like me to give you a hand with our present?' asked Stephen.

'Not yet, Stephen,' said Frankie, laughing. 'Later will be fine.'

'In that case, can I offer you a whisky?'

'Yes, thanks,' replied Frankie.

Suddenly, Angela came rushing back into the room and said, 'I forgot to tell you, Frankie, Stephen and I saw your newspaper story. It's wonderful you saved that little boy's life.'

'It was Bob Greenough's little boy who Frankie saved,' said Stephen. 'He was the jockey that died in the King's Cup a few weeks back. Poor man.'

'Oh,' said Angela, 'that's a coincidence.'

'It certainly was,' said Frankie. 'Actually, I took them both home after the accident and I've given her the rest of Mary's things.'

'Oh, that was good of you, Frankie,' said Angela. 'It must be hard without her husband to look after her and the boy. Must be hard for you too, today of all times.'

'Yes,' said Frankie, 'I hadn't expected it to be so tough. But Mary wouldn't have wanted me to mope about today.'

'No, she'd have been out playing with the children,' laughed Stephen.

Frankie took a swallow of his whisky and watched the children playing out on the lawn. 'That she would,' he said fondly, 'that she would.'

A short while later, the children were sat up at the table ready for dinner. Angela came in and placed the gravy boat on the table along with the bread sauce. Stephen went with her back into the kitchen and returned with dishes of vegetables and pointed to a seat at the other end of the table for Frankie to sit. Stephen then sat down at the opposite end and waited for Angela, who walked in carrying a dish with a huge turkey on it.

'Wow, that looks delicious,' said Frankie.

'Thank you,' said Angela.

Stephen started carving up the bird and placing slices on everyone's plates. Angela picked up the dishes containing various vegetables and put some on the children's plates. She then put some on Stephen's and her own plate and passed the dishes to Frankie to help himself. Angela then went around the table and poured gravy on the children's meals and then passed it to Frankie. When everyone had a plateful of food, Angela said grace and everyone started eating.

'Do help yourself to bread sauce, Frankie, and pass it on to Stephen,' said Angela. 'The children are not overly keen on it, it's more of an adult taste.'

'Yuck,' said one of the boys, pulling a face.

They ate in in happy conversation, Stephen and Angela sharing their favourite anecdotes about Mary, with even the children contributing. Frankie smiled to hear the stories and by the end he was beginning to feel as if she were there with them. When everyone had finished their dinner, Angela collected up the plates and carried them into the kitchen. She then came back to the table carrying a large Christmas pudding soaked in brandy and asked Stephen if he would do the honours. Stephen picked up the matches off the mantelpiece and lit the pudding. The children became excited and laughed and giggled at the sight. Angela smothered it with a cloth.

'Anything I can do, darling?' asked Stephen.

'Yes, dear, can you can get the custard and cream for me?'

Angela took a large serving spoon and put some of the pudding into three dishes for the children and placed one in front of each child. Stephen placed a jug of custard and a small dish of cream on the table.

'Here you go, Frankie,' said Angela as she passed Frankie a bowl with a large portion of pudding in. 'Help yourself to custard or cream. There's some brandy butter too.'

Angela poured a little custard on the children's puddings and told them they could begin eating. 'Now, don't forget, children, one of you will have a silver sixpence in your pudding, so don't swallow it!' All three children started dissecting their puddings until Clare gave out a shout that she had found it.

'Oh, Clare always finds it, Daddy,' said one of the boys.

'Yes,' said Stephen, 'but next year could be your turn.'

'Congratulations, Clare,' said Frankie. 'May it bring you luck all next year.'

The boys finished their pudding first and wanted to see what was in the big boxes.

'Not yet,' said Stephen. 'Not until we've all finished and the pots have been washed, then we'll open all the presents.'

When they had all finished, Angela got up from the table and started to collect the dishes.

'Can I help?' asked Frankie.

'No, you just relax, Frankie,' replied Angela.

The children jumped up from the table and ran outside to look at the boxes in the cars. Stephen poured a whisky for himself and Frankie and a large glass of wine for Angela.

'Right,' said Frankie, taking a sip of his whisky, 'shall we get the children's presents out on the lawn ready for them to open?'

Stephen agreed and they both put down their glasses and

walked out to the cars, with Angela following closely behind. First, they went to Stephen's car and lifted out the boy's boxes and put them on the lawn. Then Frankie went to his boot and got out Clare's boxes and put them on the lawn with the others.

Frankie smiled at the children. 'Stand by your boxes and when Mummy says "go" you can start opening your presents.' The three children all stood waiting for Angela to say the magic word, Frankie and Stephen turned and looked at her.

'Are you all ready?' asked Angela, giggling.

The children all shouted, 'YES!'

'GO, GO,' shouted Angela back.

The children ripped at their boxes and Clare was the first to uncover her pram. She was so excited, 'Mummy, it's just what I wanted.' Then she opened the doll. She ran up to her mother, clinging the doll to her small body, and said, 'Mummy, it's Shirley Temple! The doll all the girls at school wanted for Christmas.'

'Yes, it is and you're a very lucky girl,' said her mother.

Clare ran across the lawn, hugged Frankie and thanked him for his wonderful present. She then put her doll in her pram and started pushing it around the garden, talking to the doll as she went.

The boys were still struggling to open their presents, so Stephen and Frankie helped start them off by ripping a large piece of cardboard off their boxes. Christopher spotted the car inside and Stephen helped pull it out.

'It's a car, Daddy!' Christopher said excitedly. Stephen helped him into his car, showed him how to pedal it and off he went. Angela was helping Mark get into his red pedal car and he was soon pedalling around the garden too.

'Come and thank Uncle Frankie, boys,' said Angela.

'Thank you, Uncle Frankie,' the boys cried as they pedalled past.

'Now, I think it's your turn, Frankie,' said Stephen. The three of them walked back into the lounge and Stephen pulled out a large present from behind the settee and handed it to Frankie.

'Merry Christmas, Frankie,' said Stephen and Angela.

Frankie undid the wrapping and held up a beautiful picture of himself on a horse.

'It's me on Windsor Boy!' said Frankie.

'Yes,' said Stephen. 'The day you won the King's Cup. I looked at you coming into the winner's enclosure and thought what a wonderful idea it would be for a Christmas present. So I asked Angela to paint it for you.'

'Oh, I love it,' said Frankie. 'Angela, it's so good. You're so talented. When I get home, it's taking pride of place over the mantelpiece. Thank you both so much, I love it.'

Stephen and Angela smiled at each other.

'Now, I expect you're both anxious to see if that last box in my car is actually a safe?' said Frankie amusingly. 'I've left it until last for a specific reason and now, at two-forty-five, it's the perfect time for you both to open your present.'

'Is it a clock then?' asked Angela.

'No, it's not a clock,' said Frankie. 'You'll have to wait and see.'

Frankie looked at Stephen and said, 'Right, Stephen, I'll need your help to get the present in. It needs to go just there.' Frankie pointed to a space in the room. The two men walked out to Frankie's car and slowly pulled the big box from the back seat and carried it into the house. They placed it where Frankie had suggested and then Frankie said, 'You may now unwrap your present'.

Stephen and Angela began unwrapping the big box. Angela gave out an excited scream, 'Oh my God, it can't be?' She turned to Frankie and said, 'We can't accept this, Frankie, it's too much.'

'Of course, you can!' said Frankie. 'It's Christmas. And it's from Mary too. I want to thank you all for all that you've done for the two of us over the years, from the war onward.'

'Frankie, I don't know what to say,' said Stephen. 'It's the most wonderful gift. Angela and I will treasure it forever.'

'Well,' said Frankie, 'the reason I left it until now is so we can all sit and listen to the king's speech.' He passed Stephen the instruction pamphlet while he plugged it in. Frankie showed Stephen how to move the needle that controlled the channels and then, at three p.m. sharp, on came the king's Christmas speech.

When the programme had finished, Angela got up, looked out of the window and began to giggle.

'What is it, dear?' asked Stephen.

'Come and look, both of you,' she replied.

The two men laughed when they saw the boys washing down their cars. 'They always try and help me when I wash the car,' said Stephen, 'that's where they've got the idea from.'

Clare was still walking around the garden with her pram, talking to her new doll as she went. 'How lovely to see the children all enjoying themselves,' said Frankie.

'Would you like another whisky, Frankie, or would you prefer tea?' asked Angela.

'Oh, I would love a cup of tea,' said Frankie. 'I mustn't have too much to drink because I'm going to Shirley's later.'

The three of them sat with their teas and listened to the Christmas record Frankie had bought with the radiogram.

'Oh, it's lovely,' said Angela, singing along with the song. 'Silent night, holy night.'

'Is it Bing Crosby?' asked Stephen.

'Yes,' said Frankie, 'he is one of the most successful singers around at the moment.'

The song ended and Frankie thanked Stephen and Angela

for inviting him. He told them how much he had enjoyed the wonderful dinner and thanked them both for his lovely present that he would cherish. He picked up the painting, carried it out to his car and laid it on the back seat.

Angela called the children over to say goodbye to Frankie and thank him for his lovely presents.

'Bye, Uncle Frankie,' said the boys together, 'and thank you for our cars.'

Frankie smiled at them. 'Look after them and they will give you lots of fun.'

Clare walked up to Frankie and pulled him down so she could give him a kiss on the cheek. 'Thank you for my lovely presents,' she said. 'My friends will all be jealous when I show them Shirley Temple.'

'I'm so glad you like her,' said Frankie happily. He climbed into his car and started the engine. 'Bye then, everyone. Merry Christmas.'

They all waved as he slowly pulled away towards the main road. As he drove home, he could almost feel Mary sitting beside him, chatting about the dinner and laughing about the children's faces when they opened their presents. The thought made him smile.

Frankie arrived back at the house and parked the car. Once inside, he put his painting in the study and opened the back door. He walked over to the stable doors and opened them and brought Jennet in. Afterwards, Frankie went up the stairs to have a quick wash before he went to Shirley's. He dabbed a spot of aftershave on his chin and checked his hair in the mirror, and then walked quickly back down the stairs. He opened the front door and carried Bobby's present out to the car and placed it on the back seat. He then ran back up the steps and into the house, picked up Shirley's present and closed the front door behind him. He climbed into the car and put her present on the passenger seat next to him, and then drove off towards Shirley's.

Chapter Fifteen

Frankie woke with a start as the train juddered to a halt. His eyes snapping open, he reached for his rifle and helmet, panicking momentarily when he could not find them. It took a second for his mind to locate itself back to the train carriage, crowded with soldiers returning for leave. He glanced around embarrassed at his overreaction, but it seemed no one else had noticed or at least no one would acknowledge it – they had all been through so much.

The journey from France had been long and hard, bus from the trench, train to the port, steam ship and then a train again, day and night without stopping. Most of the uniformed men were still filthy with mud from the trenches, the stench of sweat and war laying heavy on them, but it was the smell of normality now, comforting almost. Frankie glanced around at the worn, grim faces, hollow-cheeked and red-eyed, recognising an apprehension and nervousness in their expression that mirrored his own. Guilt too, Frankie realised, a strange overwhelming guilt that had gotten worse ever since they had landed at Dover. He felt guilty being here, being safe whilst his friends were still in mortal danger, guilty that he felt resentful towards the civilians for their pampered lives. Worst of all, he felt guilty that, after all of his waiting and dreaming, he was afraid to see Mary, afraid of what she might think of the broken man he now was.

They started to disembark, a chaotic mass of limbs and kit bags. Frankie held back, letting the crowd disperse before he stepped out into the narrow corridor of the carriage. He could see them through the soot-cloud, the crowds of wives and children, waiting to welcome home their loved ones for however brief a time. He felt another pang of guilt, knowing these men were just the ghosts of those who had left, clinging to their mortal bodies but ghosts nonetheless.

He stepped down from the carriage into a cloud of smoke-soured steam and then he spotted her. Mary was wearing a stylish dress of blue-checks, cinched at the waist with a matching bow. Her brown hair was tied back in a neat bun and covered with a blue woollen hat. She didn't spot him at first and, for a second, Frankie feared he had indeed died and he was simply a spirit returning home. Part of him felt comforted by the idea.

'Frankie?' Mary almost squealed the words. She ran forwards and embraced him, her warm lips feeling alien on his own. 'Frankie, oh, Frankie.'

Frankie felt her embrace, he tried to respond but his body felt numb, sluggish. He wanted to cry, to run away. He felt so ashamed.

'What on earth has happened to you, Frankie?' asked Mary worriedly. She pulled away to inspect him, her gaze making Frankie feel filthy like some tramp or vagabond at her door, although Mary's expression showed only concern.

'Please take me home,' said Frankie quietly, his voice little more than a hoarse whisper.

Mary nodded and took his hand into her own. 'Of course, darling. Let's go home.'

The car journey was quiet. Frankie gazed out at the green, leafy, alien world outside the glass. So different from the shell-blasted, hellish landscape of the real world.

He felt a strange sense of recognition as they pulled in through the iron gates and up the gravel drive. A woman, Angela, he realised, stood waiting, smiling.

'Wait here, darling,' Mary said gently as she got out of the car. 'Help me get him into the study,' she called to Angela.

The two women helped Frankie into the house and to his armchair by the fire. Frankie allowing himself to be led, although he felt numb to it all. The room felt familiar and strange, but suddenly comforting too. Frankie thought back to those hundreds of cold, terrifying nights, when death was a screaming shell away. How he would dream of the safety of this chair, of this room and this fire. Knowing this place existed had been his armour against running away in terror.

Mary poured Frankie a whisky. He accepted it with trembling hands and downed it in one gulp, letting the fire of it burn away his shame.

'What can I do for you, Frankie?' asked Mary, stroking his face like a child.

And then Mary was there. She was really there, Frankie realised. This wasn't a dream, this was not some angel tending him on the battlefield, or some daydream. This heaven was really his home, this really was his Mary. He reached out and took her hand gently, her slender fingers felt so warm and delicate in his rough paw; pale as porcelain against the ingrained dirt of war. He was aware of her perfume too, lavender and life, pressed up against his stench of mud and death. He suddenly wanted to be clean, to be whole.

'You could run me a bath, please,' said Frankie, smiling. 'I must stink something rotten.'

Mary grinned. 'Of course, my darling. You are rather ripe.'

'I'm sorry for my behaviour, Mary. I'm...' He paused, trying to find the words. 'It's hard to believe this is real.'

'It's okay, my love,' she replied, still smiling, but Frankie could see worry in her eyes. 'You need to rest. You'll feel better after a bath and some sleep. Something to eat too.'

'I'll go and run the bath,' said Angela kindly. She left Frankie and Mary alone. The two of them keeping a sad but loving silence, Frankie unwilling to release Mary's hand.

After a few minutes, Angela shouted down that the bath was ready. Mary helped Frankie to his feet although, as they approached the doorway, Frankie started to panic, an overwhelming dread that if he left the safety of the study something terrible would happen. Mary was patient, letting him pause. Then, with the suggestion that he close his eyes, she led him up the stairs to the bedroom.

Frankie felt powerless as Mary unwrapped his mud-caked putties, eased off his boots and rolled down the filthy mass of his socks. He heard her gasp as she saw what a dreadful state his feet were in, but she said nothing that would shame him. Once she had undressed him, she helped him into the bath. It was almost uncomfortably hot, yet it felt good to feel something. Like he was a child, she washed him, draining and adding water as it blackened from the filth of war. When she was satisfied, she helped Frankie to step out of the bath, wrapped a large soft towel around him, dried him thoroughly, dressed him in his pyjamas and helped him into bed, kissing him on the forehead as she left.

'Sleep, my love, and tomorrow you'll feel better. I love you.'

As he lay there in the impossible softness, Frankie heard Mary and Angela talking downstairs. Their voices were too low to follow, but he did recognise the words 'shell shock' and knew it to be true. He hated himself for bringing the war back to this place. He wept for a while, silent, his fist to his mouth. Then, as he had done so many times before on those dark nights at the front, he slipped into sleep and the nightmares of screams and death.

***

New Square, Newbury, 1936

'Merry Christmas, Frankie,' Shirley said when she opened the door.

'Merry Christmas to you,' said Frankie, grinning. He walked into the lounge and put the big box down on the floor. 'Where's Bobby?'

'Oh, he's playing out the back,' said Shirley. She called to

Bobby from the kitchen window and he came running in excitedly from the garden.

'Merry Christmas, Bobby,' said Frankie. 'This is for you.' Frankie pointed to the big box.

Bobby's eyes lit up, his mouth opening in surprise as he ran over to the box and tried to open it. Shirley walked over and helped him. Soon the car was revealed and Bobby said, 'Wow, is it really mine, Mummy?'

'Well, yes, I suppose it is, and you must thank Mr Mills for giving you it,' said Shirley. 'You really shouldn't have, Frankie.'

Frankie smiled at Shirley. 'Please, Mary and I never had our own children. It always made us both so happy to treat the little ones of our friends.'

Shirley blushed. 'You've given us so much.'

'Thank you, Mr Frankie,' said Bobby and they all laughed.

'Oh, and this is a little something for you, Shirley,' said Frankie, handing her the gift. 'Merry Christmas.'

'Oh, Frankie, you shouldn't have. Blue Lagoon. I tried a sample in a shop a few weeks ago, I do so love lavender. It's lovely.' She walked forward and kissed Frankie on the cheek, and then applied a little to her neck. The scent bringing the presence of Mary to the room. 'Thank you. Come and have a seat by the fire.'

Bobby sat in his new car, turning the steering wheel and making racing noises. Shirley sat down in the seat opposite Frankie.

'Bobby and I have had tea, but I will make you something if you're hungry?'

'Not for me,' said Frankie, 'I'm still full from dinner.'

'Would you like a drink?' said Shirley. 'I have whisky and sherry.'

'Whisky would be fine,' said Frankie, grinning at the little boy.

Shirley poured Frankie his drink and herself a glass of sherry. They sat by the fire talking, swapping stories of horseracing and anecdotes of their late spouses. Frankie had known Bob, of course, but not well, and had always considered him a quiet man, not one for the parties and celebrations of the sport. He said as much to Shirley.

'He was much friendlier before the war,' Shirley said wistfully. 'So funny and loud. Back then he would light up a room with his jokes. When he came back... well, not all of him came back, I think.'

Frankie nodded. 'It was a dark time. It changed us all.'

'Would you tell me about the war, Frankie?' asked Bobby, looking up in sudden interest. 'Did you kill any baddies?'

Frankie felt himself flush and Shirley must have recognised his discomfort because she quickly turned to the boy.

'Bedtime now, Bobby,' said Shirley firmly.

Bobby started to cry, so Frankie said, 'Let's go up to bed and I will read you a story.'

Shirley washed Bobby, put on his pyjamas and slipped him into bed. Frankie and Shirley sat on the edge of Bobby's bed and Frankie picked up a book from the shelf.

'This is the story of Winnie the Pooh,' said Frankie. 'Once upon a time, there was a little boy named Christopher Robin and he had a little bear named Winnie the Pooh.' Shirley nudged Frankie and whispered that Bobby was already asleep. Frankie softly read another line as Shirley kissed Bobby and then he got up off the bed and put the book back on the shelf. He quietly walked out of the room and down the stairs.

Back in the lounge, Frankie said how quickly Bobby fell off to sleep. Shirley replied, 'He always does, as soon as you start reading he's fast asleep'. Frankie opened the back door and picked up a couple of logs and put them on the fire. 'I'm sorry about him asking about the war. My Bob would never talk about what he saw. I know it's hard.'

Frankie shrugged. 'Boys will always be fascinated by it. It's in our nature, but I pray to God he never need go through it. I pray we never see the like again.'

'Another drink?' asked Shirley.

'Well, I don't know if I should,' said Frankie.

'The evening's young,' said Shirley. 'We should take our joy when we can.'

'Perhaps one more would be all right,' said Frankie. The truth was he could already feel the memories creeping back up on him. That Bob had felt the same was comforting and saddening that Frankie had never had the opportunity to talk to him about it. But then he had never really spoken to anyone about it except Stephen, and he had been there.

Shirley poured Frankie a large glass of whisky and then poured herself another sherry. They sat talking for a while and then Frankie asked Shirley if she had a radio.

'We used to have one,' she said, 'but it got broken and we couldn't really afford another at the time.'

'Well,' said Frankie, 'I've just bought myself one of those new radiograms and wondered if you would like my old radio?'

'Really, you mustn't.'

'Please!' Frankie insisted. 'It's taking up space and you will be doing me a favour.'

'Then, yes please, I would,' said Shirley. 'I do miss my radio.'

'I will bring it over one day,' said Frankie.

They talked late into the evening and had drank most of the alcohol.

'I suppose I'd better think about going home,' said Frankie, rising to his feet. He swayed a little and then fell back into his chair, the action making Shirley laugh.

'You're far too tipsy to be driving, Frankie,' said Shirley with a grin. 'I'll make you a bed up on the sofa.'

'I couldn't put you to all that trouble.'

'It's no trouble at all,' replied Shirley. 'After all you've done, it's the least I could do. I'll just pop upstairs and get you a couple of blankets and a pillow.'

Frankie unfolded the blankets Shirley handed him. They smelled of soap, clean and calming. They smelled safe. He laid them across the sofa and added the pillow.

'Right,' said Shirley. 'I'll leave you to get ready for bed and see you in the morning.'

'Thanks, see you in the morning.'

Shirley disappeared up the stairs to bed. Frankie laid down on the sofa and soon slipped into a dreamless sleep.

***

'Morning, Frankie,' Shirley said as she walked towards the sofa, bright and early the next morning.

Frankie opened his eyes, confused for a moment until the events of the previous night awoke too. 'Good morning, Shirley,' he replied sleepily as Shirley placed a tray with tea and toast across his lap.

Bobby came running into the lounge and said good morning to Frankie. 'Good morning, Bobby,' said Frankie, 'and how's your little car this morning?'

'Thank you,' said Bobby, 'I love my little car. I'm just going out to have a drive in it now.'

'All right, be careful,' said Frankie. 'I will come and see you shortly.' Bobby ran off out into the garden.

'I'm sorry I couldn't afford to buy you a present, Frankie, but I'd like you to have these,' said Shirley, holding out her hand. 'They were my husband's cufflinks, which I gave him as a wedding present.'

Frankie felt the guilt again. The knowledge he had caused the man's death. They had no money because of him. Yet another debt to be repaid.

'I can't, I can't accept them,' said Frankie. 'They must be sentimental to you.'

'They will never be worn again unless you wear them,' said Shirley. 'Anyway, I want you to have them.'

Frankie looked reluctantly at the little silver links and then up at Shirley's earnest face. He could see tears at the edge of her eyes and pride there too. He knew then that she needed to give something to him. If he refused, she would be hurt, and he had already caused her enough of that.

'Well, in that case, thank you,' said Frankie. 'That's very kind of you. They really are lovely.'

They sat together but more quietly now, the two adults lost in their thoughts. Frankie feeling awkward and guilty to be there. Shirley was wearing the perfume and she smelled like Mary, it was too much.

'I really must get back to the house because of Jennet, my horse,' said Frankie.

'All right,' said Shirley, she too seemed a little relieved. 'I'll take out the tray and let you get washed and dressed.'

Frankie got up from the sofa, walked up the stairs to the bathroom and washed.

'Are you sure you can't stay, Frankie?' said Shirley.

'No, I really must go.'

Shirley's face seemed to fall a little. 'Will you be back at all? Bobby would love to see you.'

'Of course,' said Frankie, a little eagerly. 'Perhaps we might take Bobby to the park and for a little lunch.'

'Or a picnic perhaps?' said Shirley a little forcefully. She must have realised it sounded a little odd as she clarified. 'It's just that with Bob gone, money will be a little tight until I can find a job. Just a small one as we have the life insurance and his army pension, but... well... it's not a lot.'

'Well, what sort of work are you going to look for?' asked Frankie.

'Perhaps taking in washing and ironing,' she said with a shrug.

'All right then,' said Frankie, 'how about I bring you my washing once a week and leave it with you to wash and iron and pay you for the work?'

'You don't need to do that!'

Frankie placed a hand against her arm. 'Shirley, I've just lost my Mary. I'm lost without her. You would be doing me a favour.'

'Well,' said Shirley reluctantly, 'in that case, I will accept.'

'All right,' said Frankie, 'here's your first week's wages in advance.'

'That's too much, Frankie,' said Shirley.

'Take it, Shirley, please,' said Frankie. 'For you and Bobby, please. If I'd gone before my Mary, I would've wanted someone to help her, and you have little Bobby too.'

'All right,' said Shirley, thankfully. 'For Bobby.'

Frankie looked out of the kitchen window and saw Bobby driving around the garden in his little car. 'I'd better say goodbye to Bobby first.' He walked to the kitchen door and shouted, 'Bye, Bobby!'

Bobby waved at Frankie as he peddled his car around the garden, a large grin on his face.

'Right,' said Frankie, 'I'm off.'

Shirley followed Frankie to the front door and opened it.

'I will call one day with the radio and maybe we can go out for that lunch?'

'That would be nice,' Shirley said. 'See you soon, Frankie.'

Frankie walked out to the car, unlocked the door, climbed in and started the engine. 'Bye,' he said as he pulled away, waving out the window.

Shirley waved back.

Chapter Sixteen

Newbury, 1919

It had been almost five years since Frankie had driven his car. He had not felt safe to during either of his earlier visits home and even now he drove cautiously, taking the narrow country lanes slowly, being extra aware of his surroundings, being nervous of the oncoming traffic. Yet for all it scared him, Frankie found peace in driving; with his eyes and mind focussed on the road, there was no space in his brain for uninvited memories and he could tune out the phantom Germans hiding along the hedgerows.

'Such a beautiful day,' said Mary happily, glancing around at the emerald canopy that stretched over the road like a roof. 'Don't forget to turn right up ahead.'

Frankie slowed down a little more and turned into the cobbled yard of Ridgeway Stables, the grey stone buildings unchanged, the same as they had been when he had left a lifetime ago. Frankie pulled up outside the office and walked around the car to help Mary out.

Mary was dressed for the stable of course, a sturdy straight skirt, light-blue shirt and a darker blue, knitted cardigan; the spring air still having a nip of winter to it. Frankie, too, was dressed in civilian clothes and, even after a week back home, they still felt strange to him; corduroy trousers, shirt and a tweed jacket instead of his drabs. A flat cap replacing his steel Brodie helmet. By God, he felt exposed out in the open without his helmet.

'Well, well, well, would you believe it's our Frankie!' said Fred, throwing open the office door and waddling hurriedly outside. 'Good to see you, boy. Good to see you safe and well!'

Frankie held out his hand, but Fred ignored that and threw a meaty arm around him, pulling him into a rough hug that smelled of tobacco and sweat. He held the embrace a second and then stepped back to inspect Frankie.

'Did you want to check my teeth, Fred,' joked Frankie, slapping the big man on the shoulder. 'See if I'm worth buying?'

Fred laughed. 'I dunno about that, boy. I dunno whether you're fit for riding or dog meat, you look so skinny. Didn't they feed you over there?'

'Just getting down to my riding weight, Fred,' said Frankie with a grin. 'If you'll take me back?'

'Well, if you're ready to get back in the saddle, who am I to deny a bona fide war hero?'

Frankie's smile slipped for a moment. 'Don't know about that. I was just lucky is all.'

'I know, and we're lucky to have you home, boy,' replied Fred solemnly. 'Did you hear Bill Townsend's son, Amos, didn't come home. He joined up a year after you. Lost at the Somme.'

Frankie nodded slowly. If he closed his eyes he could again see the sea of mud and corpses that the battle became, he could hear the guns and the screams and the begging of dying men. 'Too many lost there.'

'Aye,' replied Fred. Suddenly, he brightened. 'Well, that's all in the past, isn't it? You're home safe now and, if you can get your strength up, you can start back in a fortnight. Get you racing, huh? And your job, young Mary, is to feed him up!'

'I will,' giggled Mary.

'Um... so we have some more news,' said Frankie. 'Mary?'

Mary lifted her left hand to show a golden ring. 'Frankie proposed.'

'And we have a little question to ask,' said Frankie.

'Would you give me away? Please?' asked Mary. 'There's no one else we would want to do it.'

Fred's grin could not have been any wider as he grabbed them both into his warm hug. His voice choked with emotion as he replied.

'Of course, I will. Of course! My babies, of course, I will.'

***

Speen Moor Manor, Newbury, 1936

Frankie pulled up outside the manor, opened the front door and walked inside. *I suppose I had better check on Jennet first*, he thought. He opened the back door and walked out to the stable. Frankie greeted Jennet with a pat.

'Hello, old girl, did you miss me?' Frankie led her out and walked her to the paddock. He opened the gate, took the lead off and let her run out into the field. 'And don't go jumping the fence again,' Frankie shouted to her as she ran off in that direction.

He walked to the shed and fetched the tools to put his new painting up over the fireplace; that done, he stood back and stared at the picture for a minute. It was a beautiful image, no doubt. Angela had captured the moment perfectly, the drama, the excitement of the win. And yet... and yet Frankie could not forget that only moments later he would learn that Bob was dead, dead because of his actions. A prelude to the spiral of events that led to this place, to him alone and Mary gone.

Suddenly, he went to take it down, to get it out of his study, his refuge against the world. He wanted to smash it up and burn it on the fire, to destroy that moment and all the memories. He wanted to forget. No, he was desperate to forget what he had done to Bob, to Mary, to Shirley and little Bobby too, to the homeless man who had taken the blame, and even, as much as it pained him, to forget what he had done to Ernie. He reached up to pull it down and then he stopped himself. Angela had given it to him and he couldn't let her down. *Besides*, he thought to himself, *it's right I should always be reminded, that I should never be allowed to forget. The painting is my punishment, my purgatory.*

Frankie poured himself a whisky and downed it fast, pouring

another. He kept his eyes low, away from the mantle and the image. *Hubris,* Frankie thought sardonically. *The Greeks would have called that moment 'hubris' and blamed me for what happened.* He downed the second whisky. *I have to get out. I'll go to the café. I need to get out.*

Frankie slammed the glass down, put on his hat and coat and drove into town.

Frankie walked into the café and was welcomed by the waitress. 'Hello, Mr Mills.'

'Hello,' said Frankie, forcing an unconvincing smile. The waitress walked him over to a table at the back of the café.

'Your usual, Mr Mills?' asked the waitress.

'Yes,' said Frankie, distractedly. 'And a pot of tea, please.'

'Didn't expect to see you today,' said the waitress. 'We don't get a lot of business on Boxing Day. Tends to be travellers more than anything.'

Frankie shrugged. 'I didn't feel like being alone at home. Too many ghosts this time of year.'

The waitress smiled at him sadly and left with the order. She returned moments later and put the tray on the table. Frankie poured himself a cup and sat looking out of the window, dreaming of past visits, when the girl returned again with his meal.

'I meant to say I heard that poor man died,' said the waitress.

'What poor man?' asked Frankie, dreading the answer.

'You know, the man from the house fire. He was in a coma.'

'What?' said Frankie, in surprise. 'From the other day.'

'Yes, that's the one,' replied the girl. 'Cook told me his name was Ernie Keep. Apparently, he was a groundsman at the racecourse. Cook says the paper said he never woke up, poor thing. What a way to go.'

Frankie's heart was pounding now. He felt something, a sudden lightness. Was that relief? A lifting of the burden of hate and injustice. Ernie was dead and he had deserved to die. He had deserved it a hundred times over and now Frankie was in the clear. He still needed to make it right by Shirley, but he was free of the blackmailer.

'Are you okay, Mr Mills?'

Frankie realised he had been silent too long. He needed to say something to explain it.

'It's just... I knew Ernie Keep,' said Frankie. 'We served together in the war. My God.'

'I'm so sorry,' said the girl. 'Sorry to bring bad news.'

'Oh, Ernie wasn't a good man,' replied Frankie. He realised this too sounded suspicious. 'I mean, he didn't deserve this though. Did the cook say what the police are thinking?'

She shrugged. 'I don't know. It's probably an accident.'

'Probably,' replied Frankie. 'Thank you for the meal.'

The waitress smiled and nodded, then turned and walked back to the kitchen, leaving Frankie alone.

He finished his lunch, paid the waitress and gave her a tip.

'Thank you, Mr Mills,' said the girl as Frankie walked to the door, feeling a lightness that had not been there before.

Outside, it had started to rain again, so Frankie raced back to the house to get Jennet in. He pulled up outside and quickly ran up the steps and opened the door. He walked straight through the house and out the back door to the yard, along the muddy path to the paddock and there stood Jennet at the gate. Frankie led her back to her stable and gave her a thorough rub down. He checked her feed and water and gave her a pat. Then he shut the doors and walked back into the house.

In the study, Frankie made up a fire and lit it. He poured himself a whisky and sat down in his armchair, avoiding looking up at the painting. *Looks like I need some more logs chopping*, he thought. *It'll have to wait until this rain stops though*. Frankie turned on the radiogram and started playing his records, anything to drown out his thoughts. He sat listening for a while, when the phone rang.

'Hello,' said Frankie.

'Is that Mr Mills?'

'Yes,' replied Frankie.

'It's Police Inspector George Allen here,' came the gruff voice.

'Oh, hello, Inspector,' said Frankie with an affected cheerfulness. 'How can I help you?'

'Well, I'm just phoning ahead of the pre-trial in two days'

time for your late-wife's case. I wanted to check you'll still be attending.'

'Yes, I'll be there. Has he confessed?'

'No,' said the inspector. 'No, he still insists he's innocent. It's going to be a lot harder for us to get a conviction without a confession. We know he did it, but the evidence isn't strong. Of course, we'll do our very best.'

'Thank you, Inspector. I understand you're doing all you can.'

The inspector provided the details and times and Frankie thanked him before returning the receiver. *The evidence is weak,* thought Frankie happily. *If he gets off, then this is all over. It'll all be over.* His eye fell on the painting and he knew it would never truly be over. He decided he needed to call Stephen.

'Hello,' said Frankie when Stephen answered the phone.

'Hello, Frankie, how are you? Thank you for the radiogram. You really shouldn't have, but she is an absolute beauty. The sound is wonderful.'

'It is, isn't it. I was just listening to mine. Perhaps we'll have to swap records some time.'

'Well, you're welcome to keep the Shirley Temple one that Clare keeps making me play. I swear if I hear about the lollipop ship one more time I may well go crazy.'

Frankie laughed. 'Well, I'm yet to experience that. Stephen, the reason I'm calling is because the pre-trial for Mary's case is in two days' time in Reading and I wondered if you'd like to come along with me?'

'Of course, I will.'

'Only if you're sure though,' said Frankie. 'Are you not riding that day?'

'No,' said Stephen, 'I've still got three days' holiday left before returning to the track.'

'Well, it would be nice to have you along,' said Frankie.

'What time would you like me to arrive then?'

'Well, I was thinking of leaving around nine-thirty,' said Frankie.

'All right, your place at nine-thirty a.m., two days from now,' said Stephen. 'Angela sends her love and the children haven't stopped playing with their gifts you gave them for Christmas.'

'I'm glad they liked them,' said Frankie, 'and please give my regards to Angela.'

'I will,' said Stephen. 'Bye, Frankie.'

'Bye, Stephen.'

Frankie put down the phone and returned to his chair. *It is nearly all over now.*

Chapter Seventeen

Speen Moor Manor, Newbury, 1919

'My grandmother always used to say marrying in June makes for a happy marriage,' said Angela happily. 'Because Juno was the Roman goddess who watched over women's lives and she's also the goddess of love and marriage.'

'Then it's meant to be,' added Stephen, raising his pint glass and winking at Angela as they toasted the soon-to-be newlyweds.

Frankie caught the gesture and smiled. He knew Stephen and Angela had met up a few times when Stephen had been on leave. They made a good couple, he reckoned. Stephen was like a brother to him now, after all they had been through, and Angela was like sister to Mary. Maybe that, too, was meant to be.

'So, will our handsome former soldiers be wearing their uniforms to the wedding?' asked Angela.

Frankie felt his stomach knot at the thought of putting on drabs again. Stephen caught his expression and laughed.

'No fear!' Stephen said a little too loudly and Frankie knew it was to protect him. 'Besides, Frankie here wouldn't be happy with me outranking him again.'

'Stop it,' Mary giggled, slapping Stephen's arm playfully. 'No, Angela, they've both splashed out on lovely new suits. And anyway, you might have more stripes, Stephen Sheehan, but Frankie is the groom and so tomorrow, at least, he outranks you.'

'He's got more medals too,' rumbled Fred. 'Proper hero, our Frankie.'

It was an awkward thing to say. Normally, talk of medals would send Frankie back to the dark thoughts, as Mary and Stephen both well knew. *But not today,* Frankie thought; today Frankie was determined to leave the war in France and so, with an effort of will, he pushed the memories back down deep. Still, as always, Stephen stepped in to lighten the mood.

'Doesn't change the fact I'm officially the best man though,' replied Stephen. 'And I think you'll find this particular rank makes me the very best man at the wedding!' He winked at Angela, who blew him a kiss.

Frankie grinned at his companions. These five people were more than friends, they were his family and he loved them all. He glanced over to Mary, as beautiful as he had ever seen her, her skin pale in the low light of the pub, her lips a vibrant red and her eyes glittering with laughter. She saw him looking at her and smiled back, that dazzling smile that had first caught his eye, and Frankie's heart leapt. He knew now more than ever she was his world, his everything, and for as long as he had her, he could fight the descent into those memories, he could hold the horrors at bay.

The wedding had been a true labour of love. Frankie had reserved Saint Mary the Virgin's little church and he and

Mary had decided to have the wedding reception in the paddock. They had hired a large marquee and the catering would be provided by a local company. Fred, himself, had been busily refurbishing his old carriage and it now gleamed white, and he and Frankie had spent the past few hours wiring flowers to the wheels. Mary would arrive to her wedding like a princess.

'Last orders, gentleman!' the call went out from the bar.

Stephen looked at his wristwatch. 'It's only nine-thirty.'

'Worst bit about the war,' said Fred, winking at Frankie. 'This early closing bit lingering on. That and them watches on your arm like lady's wristlets. A real man wears his watch on a chain.'

Stephen grinned. 'You try opening a fancy watch case in a trench. It'll be bunged up in mud in no time.'

Fred shook his head. 'All getting too fast, this modern world. All these cars and flying plane things, and everyone stuck to a radio. You know my missis is having a telephone installed in my office now? A telephone! Why do I want that? What's wrong with just talking to someone face to face. I don't want to be chased up by every Tom, Dick and Harry whenever they feel like it.'

'Okay, Grandad,' laughed Stephen. 'Can I get anyone a last drink.'

Angela emptied her glass and stood up. 'No, you boys stay. Mary and I need to head off and get ready. One of us is getting married in the morning. Besides, you shouldn't have even been seeing each other tonight.'

'I spent four years not seeing Frankie each night,' said Mary reaching over and gripping his hand. 'I'm not going to let superstition rob me of more.'

'Besides,' said Stephen, 'these two are meant to be. There's no bad luck going to keep them apart.'

***

Speen Moor Manor, Newbury, 1936

Frankie climbed out of bed and walked into the bathroom to run a bath. When it had filled to halfway, he climbed in and slowly sat down in the water. He turned off the cold tap, but left the hot tap running until he felt it was hot enough. Frankie washed himself, all the time thinking of what he had to do that day. *I must give the radio a quick clean before I take it to Shirley's and I must phone the solicitor first thing*.

Frankie finished his bath, climbed out and dried himself. He put on his dressing gown and slippers and walked downstairs. *It's cold down here this morning*, he thought, *must have been a frost overnight*. He went into the study, avoiding contact with the painting, screwed up some newspapers and put them in the grate. He then added some kindling wood and lit the paper. While the fire was starting to catch, Frankie walked into the kitchen and put on the kettle to make a cup of tea. Meanwhile he quickly went back into the study and put two logs on the fire. He turned on the radio and sat listening to it for a while, and then went upstairs and shaved, dressed and returned to the study.

Frankie took his address book from the bureau drawer and looked for the solicitor's phone number. Frankie dialled the number and the receptionist answered, 'Good morning, Adams and Co solicitors.'

'Oh, good morning,' said Frankie. 'I wasn't sure if you were back at work yet after the Christmas break.'

'Oh, yes,' said the woman, 'we came back this morning.'

'My name is Frankie Mills,' said Frankie, 'and I wish to add something to my will. I wondered if Richard could fit me in quickly today?'

'Hold on, Mr Mills, I'll just call through to him.' Moments later, the woman answered and told Frankie there was a fifteen-minute gap at ten-forty-five if he could make it.

'Yes, that'll be just fine,' said Frankie. 'I'll see you then.'

Frankie put down the phone and made a mental note of the ten-forty-five appointment at the solicitors. He lifted the radio down from the shelf and carried it through to the kitchen. He rinsed out a damp cloth and gave the radio exterior a quick wipe over. He then dried it with a soft cloth and it almost looked brand new. *That's come up looking really nice*, he thought.

He took a clothes brush from a drawer and gave himself a quick brush down before polishing his shoes. When he was satisfied he looked all right, he returned to the study and turned off the radiogram, again his face averted from the painting hanging accusingly over the fireplace. *I don't know if I can bear this,* he thought sadly. *Mary, I wish you were here.*

Frankie walked along the hall to the stand and took down his hat and coat. Opening the front door, Frankie stopped for a moment to see if he had forgotten anything. For a moment, he imagined he could hear Mary calling from the kitchen but he knew it was in his mind. He closed the door and walked down the steps to the car.

When he arrived at the solicitors' office, the receptionist greeted him and asked him to go straight in as Richard, his solicitor, was free. Frankie walked along to the man's door and knocked.

'Come in,' said a voice. Frankie opened the door and walked in. The man behind the desk was immaculately dressed, he stood up stiffly and held out his hand to shake Frankie's. 'Good morning, Mr Mills, and what can I do for you today?'

'Well,' said Frankie, 'I just want to add one thing to my will.'

'I see, Mr Mills, and what would you like to add?'

'I want Mrs Shirley Greenough of One New Square, Newbury, to have the first one-hundred pounds of my estate,' said Frankie.

Richard nodded and then folded himself neatly into his stuffed leather chair, gesturing for Frankie to do the same.

'Well, that's straight forward enough, Mr Mills. I think we can quickly do that now.'

Richard called the receptionist to bring Frankie's will into the office and added what Frankie had asked to it. When he had done, the solicitor and the receptionist witnessed it and asked Frankie to sign it to make it legal.

'That's that then,' said the solicitor. 'All taken care of Mr Mills.'

Frankie thanked him for seeing him at such short notice and shook his hand again before being shown out by the receptionist.

Back in the car, Frankie drove along the road to the little florist shop. He looked in the window at all the different flowers and walked in.

'Good morning, sir,' said the lady inside. 'How can I help you?'

'I'm looking for a lovely bunch of flowers,' said Frankie. 'For a friend.'

'We've some beautiful yellow roses in,' said the woman, gesturing to a display. 'Hot house grown, just in this morning.'

'They are absolutely perfect,' said Frankie. He remembered wistfully how he would come in here to buy carnations for Mary; she would have loved the yellow roses. 'I'll take a bunch of those, please.'

'Certainly, sir,' said the woman. She carefully wrapped the stems in tissue paper and handed them to Frankie.

'Thank you very much,' said Frankie, walking to the door.

As he walked back up the street, Frankie remembered little Bobby and so he called in at the sweet shop and bought Bobby a big bag of sweets. *Right, that's it*, thought Frankie. He caught a glance at the display for the new Dairy Box chocolates, thinking suddenly of how he had bought some for Mary only a few months before and how she had squealed with excitement at the gift. He loved it when he could make Mary smile.

'Are you okay, sir?' asked the counter assistant.

Frankie realised he must have been standing there for a while. He smiled at the girl.

'Just thinking about how much my wife enjoys them,' he said, pointing to the chocolates.

'Yes, they're very popular,' said the girl. 'Would you like one for her?'

'Yes. Yes, please,' said Frankie, pulling out his wallet again.

He made his way back to where the car was parked. He opened the door and laid the flowers and sweets on the passenger seat next to him and stared at the chocolates. What had he been thinking? He had bought them for Mary, but that made no sense. He could hardly give them to Shirley, not with flowers too; she might get the wrong idea and they had both been widowed only recently. Angela, he would give them to Angela.

Frankie started the engine and slowly drove away in the direction of Shirley's house. When he arrived, he climbed out of his car with the bunch of flowers and the sweets, tucking the chocolates beneath the seat where they would not be seen. Frankie walked along the alley to Shirley's house, she was outside and came over to greet Frankie.

'Are they for me?' She accepted them and sniffed at the blooms. 'They're beautiful, thank you.'

Frankie passed the sweets too. 'And these are for Bobby. Go on in,' he said. 'I'll just be a moment. I've got to get the radio from the car and then I'll be back.'

Frankie returned to the car and lifted out the radio, pushing the door shut with his leg. He carried the radio to the house and put it on the table in the lounge. Shirley came in from the back garden with an already sticky Bobby and Frankie showed them the radio. Shirley pointed to where he could plug it in. Frankie turned it on and the music started to play.

'Oh, it's wonderful to have music back in the house,' said Shirley. 'Thank Frankie for your sweets, Bobby.'

'Thank you very much, Mr Frankie,' said Bobby, his mouth filled with sugar.

Shirley returned from the kitchen with the roses in a tall vase and put it on the table. 'Mmmn,' said Shirley, again smelling the perfume from the roses. 'They really are beautiful.'

'You'd better keep some of those sweets for later, Bobby,' Frankie said. 'Otherwise, they may spoil your dinner.'

Frankie turned to Shirley and asked, 'I wondered if you and Bobby would like to come out for dinner?'

'Are you sure, Frankie? Haven't you had enough of us?'

Frankie shook his head. 'Please, I'd love the company.'

'We would love to then, wouldn't we, Bobby?' said Shirley, nodding to the boy who was just popping another jelly into his mouth. The little boy nodded eagerly.

Shirley took Bobby upstairs to wash his hands and face and put on his best clothes. When she came back downstairs, she was wearing one of Mary's dresses, the lavender scent of her perfume preceding her. For a second, Frankie only saw Mary; his mouth going dry and his heart hammering as Mary smiled at him with her sparkling doe eyes. He blinked and Mary was gone, a smiling Shirley looking at him instead.

'Would it be all right, Frankie, if I wore this lovely dress of Mary's today? I don't want to upset you.'

'You look beautiful, Mary, err, Shirley, and no I would love you to wear it. I'm sure Mary would be pleased someone else loved it as much as she did.' He looked up at her again, hoping against reason to see Mary, but it was only Shirley. He forced a smile. 'Okay, off we go.'

Shirley took Bobby's hand and followed Frankie out to the car.

'You can sit in the front with Bobby or in the back, it's up to you,' said Frankie.

Bobby said he wanted to sit up in the front, so Shirley opened the front passenger door and got in with Bobby on her lap, the smell of her perfume filling the space and making Frankie smile. He started the engine, tooted his horn and off they went.

Bobby was excited, pointing out everything as they drove along the road towards the café.

'Here we are,' said Frankie as they pulled up outside. He got out and walked around to the passenger side and opened the door for Shirley and Bobby. The three of them walked across the car park to the café and Frankie opened the door for them to walk in.

'Hello, Mr Mills,' said the waitress. 'Back again.'

'Table for three, please,' said Frankie. 'Yes, of course, there is no finer place in all of Newbury.'

The waitress grinned and showed them to a table.

'Here you are, Shirley, choose something for yourself and Bobby,' said Frankie, handing the menu over to Shirley. 'I'll have the fish today.'

'Yes, Mr Mills,' said the waitress.

'I'll have the same,' said Shirley, 'and a small portion for Bobby please.'

'And would you like a pot of tea, sir, while you're waiting?'

'Yes, please,' said Frankie. 'For two, and a pop for Bobby.'

The girl walked off to the kitchen and Frankie took off his hat and coat and hung it up on the stand. The girl returned with a pot of tea and put it on the table.

'This is nice, isn't it, Bobby?' asked Shirley.

'Yes, Mummy,' said Bobby.

The girl returned and put the glass of lemonade on the table in front of Bobby. He picked it up, drank half of it and put it back on the table.

'Mmmn,' said Bobby, 'I was thirsty, Mummy.'

A few minutes passed and the waitress returned with their meals on a tray. She placed the plates in front of everyone.

'Thank you,' said Frankie.

Bobby picked up his knife and fork and wasted no time in tucking in to his dinner. The three of them sat enjoying their meals and Frankie asked if they would like to come back to his house and see his horse.

'Oh, that would be lovely, Frankie,' said Shirley.

'A horse?' asked Bobby excitedly.

'Yes,' said Frankie, 'my horse is called Jennet.'

They finished their dinner and the waitress asked if they would like dessert.

'Can I have the fruit and ice-cream, please?' asked Shirley.

'Certainly,' said Frankie. 'How about you, Bobby, would you like some too?'

'Yes, please, Mr Frankie,' said Bobby happily.

'I'll have the same please,' said Frankie.

The waitress went back to the kitchen to fetch their desserts. The girl returned with three bowls of fruit and ice-cream and placed them on the table.

'Mmmn,' said Bobby, licking his lips. Shirley handed Bobby his spoon and he started eating.

'Oh, that's wonderful,' said Shirley, 'I do love ice-cream.'

Frankie smiled again. Mary had loved ice-cream too. He thought wistfully of a world where the two of them would be sat here with a child, enjoying a meal. It was not meant to be though.

They finished their desserts and Frankie paid the bill and gave the girl her tip.

'Thank you very much,' said the waitress. 'Have a lovely day.'

Frankie got up from the table and pulled Shirley's chair back so she could get out and help Bobby down from his seat. Frankie led the way to the door and the three of them walked out into the carpark.

'I thought we might just have a few minutes by the river before we go back to my house,' said Frankie.

'Yes, that would be nice,' said Shirley. 'Blow out some cobwebs.'

They walked across the bridge and down to the river's edge.

'Now, Bobby,' said Frankie, 'you must never walk too close to the edge, otherwise you could fall in like you did before. When you are older, you must learn to swim, and when you do, you must move your arms like this.' Frankie demonstrated how to move your arms to do the breast stroke. 'And then you must kick your legs like this,' said Frankie, again demonstrating how to do it.

Shirley giggled at Bobby trying to copy Frankie. 'I will make sure he learns when he is old enough.'

They walked along the riverbank watching the swans and

ducks sailing up and down the river for a while until Bobby said he wanted to use the bathroom.

'There's a toilet over there where Mummy can take you,' said Frankie.

They walked over the grass to the toilet and Shirley took him into the ladies. A few minutes later, Shirley and Bobby came out and the three of them walked back along the river path to the bridge and crossed it to the carpark. Bobby spotted Frankie's car and went running on ahead.

'Wait for us,' said Shirley. The three of them got into the car and Frankie drove slowly back home.

'Here we are,' said Frankie as he pulled up outside Speen Moor Manor.

'Looks lovely, Frankie,' said Shirley admiringly. 'I bet the flowers look glorious in the summer. Oh, and the views.'

Frankie led the way up the steps and unlocked the front door. He walked in and took off his hat and coat and hung them up.

'Can I take your coat?' Frankie asked Shirley.

'Yes, thank you,' said Shirley, slipping out of her coat.

He took them both into the study and sat them down on the sofa. 'I'll make up a fire,' he said and he took out some newspapers, screwed them up and placed them in the grate. He then added some kindling wood and lit it. 'There we are. I'll just give it a minute to get going and then I'll add a couple of logs. Now, how about a nice cup of tea?'

'Yes, I'd love a cup', said Shirley, 'and something for Bobby, please'.

Frankie showed Shirley his new radiogram and he put on the records he had bought. He walked into the kitchen, made Bobby a drink and took it into him. Then he returned with a cup of tea each for Shirley and himself.

'Thank you,' said Shirley, taking the cup from Frankie. Shirley was looking at the painting of Frankie over the fireplace. 'Wasn't that the race that Bob was—'

'Yes,' Frankie quickly stopped her mid-sentence. 'I'm sorry, it was a Christmas present from my friend who's also a jockey. To be honest, it makes me feel awful. I'll take it down if it upsets you?'

'No, Frankie, it's fine. It wasn't your fault. It really isn't, please don't blame yourself. They should never have let the race happen in that fog. They should have delayed it or cancelled it...' Shirley took a deep breath and wiped away a tear. 'I'm sorry, Frankie. It's just still so raw, and with Christmas and everything...'

'I know,' said Frankie, fighting back tears of his own. 'That's how I feel about Mary. I feel like I'm in a daze most of the time. I keep expecting her to come through the door or to call from the kitchen. I just can't really believe she's gone.'

Shirley placed a comforting hand against Frankie's arm. 'She's not gone, Frankie. She's still here. I can feel her love in this room.' She smiled at him sadly and Frankie could hear Mary in her words.

'Where's the horse, Frankie?' asked Bobby suddenly.

'Oh, she's out in the stable,' said Frankie, shaking his head to drive away the sadness. 'Shall we go and see her?'

'Yes, please, Mr Frankie,' said Bobby.

Frankie led the way to the back door, unlocked it and walked down the steps to the stable. He opened up both of the doors and there stood Jennet drinking from her trough.

'Hello, Jennet,' said Frankie, giving her a pat. 'I've bought someone to see you.'

Frankie lifted Bobby up, sat him on Jennet's back and held on to him.

'Be careful, Frankie,' said Shirley worryingly.

'Oh, he's fine as long as I've got hold of him,' said Frankie. 'Do you like her, Bobby?'

'I'm like Daddy,' said Bobby.

Frankie looked over towards Shirley who had gone pale-faced.

'You are,' said Frankie gently. 'Your daddy was the best jockey I ever raced against.'

Frankie lifted him down and told them he would be back in a moment. He walked into the kitchen and came back out with some sugar knobs in his hand.

'Here you are, Bobby, give Jennet some sugar like this.' He held out Bobby's hand flat for Jennet to take the sugar.

'It tickles,' said Bobby laughing.

'Yes, that's her whiskers,' said Frankie.

'How about Mummy?' asked Bobby. 'Do you want to give Jennet some sugar?'

Shirley seemed to have recovered herself. She smiled and held out her hand as Frankie put a sugar lump on it. Jennet sucked it up from her palm.

Shirley laughed. 'It really does tickle, doesn't it, Bobby?'

'I told you, Mummy!' the little boy said, smiling at his mother.

'Well, it's time for Jennet's sleepy byes,' said Frankie, 'so say goodnight, Bobby.'

Bobby said goodnight to Jennet. Frankie closed up the doors and the three of them went back into the house. The fire was still burning so Frankie took Shirley and Bobby on a tour of the house.

'Oh, it's wonderful,' said Shirley. 'What a lovely house.'

Frankie took them both back down stairs and put the records on again for them to listen to. They danced and played with Bobby for a while until Shirley suggested it was getting time for them to go.

'I suppose,' said Frankie reluctantly. 'I'll grab our coats and drive you back.'

'Thank you, Frankie.'

'Actually, I've got to go to Reading tomorrow for the hearing of the man accused of Mary's murder, to see if there's enough evidence for a trial,' he said quietly to Shirley.

'My goodness, I didn't realise they'd caught someone already.'

'Yes,' said Frankie sadly, 'but the man is pleading not guilty. In all truth, I don't know if he's the one but we'll soon know. I'll let you know how things go.'

'Yes, please do, Frankie. Please let me know if there is anything I can do.'

Frankie opened the door and waited while Shirley and Bobby walked down the steps to the car. He locked the front door and opened the passenger side for Shirley and Bobby to get in. He shut their door, walked around the car and climbed in behind the wheel.

'Everybody ready?' he said, 'then off we go.' The car slowly pulled away and Frankie tooted his horn. 'Here you are, Bobby. You have a go.'

Bobby pushed the horn a couple of times and laughed with excitement. 'Beep, Beep,' said Bobby as they drove along.

After a quarter of an hour, Frankie pulled up outside Shirley's house. 'Here we are,' he said. He got out of the car and walked around and let Shirley and Bobby out. She walked up the alley to the front door and opened it.

'Coming in, Frankie?' asked Shirley, looking back at Frankie following behind with Bobby.

Frankie shook his head. 'I really must be going now.' He wanted to go in, to be with this little family, but knew if he did he might never leave. 'I'll call in on my way back from the court.'

'I'll see you tomorrow then, Frankie,' Shirley replied.

'Bye,' said Frankie. He climbed into his car and waved to Shirley at the door as he pulled away. Frankie drove home happier than he had been for quite a while.

He pulled up outside his house, retrieved the chocolates from under the seat and walked up the steps to the door. The phone was ringing, so Frankie quickly shut the door and walked into the study. The room smelled faintly of lavender still and Frankie breathed it in deeply. Dropping the chocolates on the side table for Mary later, he picked up the phone.

'Hello,' said Frankie.

'Hello, Frankie, it's Angela. I've been trying to contact you for ages.' Angela's voice was emotional.

'Is everything okay?'

'Well, no, not really, Frankie. Stephen was taken ill during the night and I had to call out the doctor. He has pneumonia and he's in the hospital. They say he'll be all right because he's young and fit but, of course, it means he won't be able to come with you tomorrow. I'm sorry, Frankie.'

'Please don't worry, Angela. Thanks for letting me know. Tell Stephen to concentrate on getting better. I'll take Mary. I'll phone you when I get back from Reading to see how things are going. If there's anything we can do, please don't hesitate to ask.'

'Mary, Frankie?' said Angela uncertainly.

'No,' replied Frankie, feeling confused. 'Of course, not. Sorry, it's all a bit much today.'

'Are you okay, Frankie?' asked Angela. 'Do you want to come here?'

'No, no, I'm okay, just a bit tired. Send Stephen my love, please. And thank you for everything you two have done for Mary and I, it means everything to me.'

'Okay,' said Angela reluctantly. 'Well, I have to go, I've got to get a message to Stephen's mother, but do let me know if you do need anything, Frankie. I hope it goes well tomorrow.'

'Bye,' said Frankie, putting down the phone.

Chapter Eighteen

Speen Moor Manor, Newbury, 1919

Frankie looked out over the busy paddock. The off-white marquee was up and people were scurrying around laying out tables and chairs around the paddock for people to sit out in the sunshine if they wished. The whole field had been decorated with garlands of flowers and streamers of ribbon, and each table had a small bouquet of flowers. It was perfect, and Mary deserved perfection.

Frankie smiled as he stepped back into the house, deliberately ignoring the phantom German soldiers he had spotted lurking in the small copse at the back. Today was not a day for hallucinations, today was a day for celebration and for the future, not the past.

'Shouldn't you be getting yourself ready?' called Edith, Fred's wife, as Frankie slipped past. Edith had insisted on making the cake, a magnificent two-tiered confection of sugar flowers and icing. She picked up the little pottery groom figure and waggled it at him accusingly. 'Your Mary will be being primped and painted to within an inch of her life right now, so the least you can do is be ready on time!'

Frankie laughed and saluted, dashing up the stairs to the bedroom where Stephen was almost ready.

'Come on, man, we're going to be late. And I'm not prepared to take the blame for your sluggishness!'

Frankie dressed quickly, with Stephen coming over to help him with his jacket.

'Not bad if I do say so myself,' said Stephen cheerfully. 'We might just get away with this, old boy.'

Frankie looked at himself in the long mirror Mary had brought from her parent's house when she had moved in. He really did feel he looked pretty handsome in his navy-blue three-piece suit and black brogue shoes polished to a military shine. He wore a blue patterned tie and Stephen was just tucking a large white gardenia into his buttonhole.

'You know, I'm as nervous as I've ever been,' said Frankie. 'I think I was less nervous waiting for the whistle at the Somme.'

'Then you're a better man than me,' laughed Stephen. 'I was trembling so hard I'm surprised my helmet wasn't ringing like a bell. Besides, what do you have to be nervous about? You two are made for each other.'

'That I'll let Mary down,' said Frankie, suddenly serious. 'I still get the nightmares, Stephen. I still jump when I hear a bang or panic at a shadow, and I still wake up in the trenches every night with the flare going over.'

'It's only been a little while, Frankie. I always see the lads we lost, poor Alfie in that shell hole or Sarge just before the shell. I was talking to him not five minutes before you know. Scares me how close it was. But it will get better, with time.'

'Thank you, Stephen. You know I couldn't have got through all this without you.'

Stephen laughed in embarrassment. 'Save some romance for Mary. Now, are you fit?'

'I think I'm as ready as I'm ever going to be.' He looked at his watch and saw it was just past two. 'I will just check one last time that everything is in place in the paddock and we will get off.'

The two men left the room and returned downstairs, quickly walking around to check everything was ready.

'Come on, Frankie. It's two-fifteen,' said Stephen impatiently.

'All right, I think it's all ready. Come on then, let's go. It's only a short drive up the road.'

The two men jumped into Frankie's car and sped off down the road towards the little Saxon church. Parking in the lane, Frankie gave Stephen the keys to the car. They brushed themselves down and strolled into the church, passing the Lady's Well as they did so. Frankie took a sixpence from his pocket and cast it into the waters, making a silent wish for a long and happy marriage. They walked into the packed church and made their way down the narrow aisle to the front, stopping along the way to greet and thank the congregation who had come to see them.

Frankie was nervous as they waited. Twice he asked Stephen if he had the ring and twice the exasperated Stephen replied, 'Yes, Frankie, it's right here,' tapping theatrically at his pocket.

'Do try and relax,' said Stephen. 'It'll all be over soon.'

There was a sudden commotion at the end of the church. Someone at the door nodded to the vicar, who in turn signalled to the organist to start playing the wedding march. Frankie felt himself shaking and it must have been enough for Stephen to see.

'Stay calm, Frankie, here she comes,' whispered Stephen.

And then Mary was walking down the aisle on Fred's arm, with Angela walking about three yards behind carrying Mary's long train. Frankie watched in rapt awe as she approached, an angelic vision more stunning than anything he had dreamt of in the lonely horrors of the war. The beautiful silk wedding dress was decorated with ornate beading on the bodice and bordered with sprays of orange blossom to match her orange blossom coronet. Mary held a large bouquet of white narcissus, rosebuds and lily of the valley with long white silk ribbons hanging down to the ground. She passed the flowers to Angela as she stopped at Frankie's side. Frankie lifted the veil to reveal her beautiful face.

'I love you,' she said as Frankie grinned at her.

'I love you too,' replied Frankie happily.

***

Speen Moor Manor, Newbury, 1936

At seven-thirty a.m., the alarm went off and Frankie reached over and hit the button to stop the noise. The truth was he had barely slept. His night had been disturbed with memories and nightmares, all mixed together in a chaotic vision. He had been back at Loos, only Mary had been there and he had been desperate to get her to safety before they went over the top. Then he had been in a burning farmhouse, pulling the blackened corpses of Shirley and Bobby from the ash, all the while ignoring Ernie who had taunted and jeered. There had been so many more dark and half-forgotten horrors that were real memories and others that could not be.

He pulled the covers back and slowly got up from the bed, scratching at his face. He put on his dressing gown and slippers and walked into the bathroom. He put the plug in the sink and turned on the cold tap, splashing his face to cleanse the dreams. He washed and shaved and returned to the bedroom where he dressed in his white shirt and best suit and walked down the stairs.

In the kitchen, Frankie filled the kettle and put it on the stove to boil. He made himself a cup of tea and two slices of toast, and took them into the study, again not looking at the picture over the fire. Mary's chocolates were still on the table untouched and, for a moment, Frankie was surprised she had not eaten them.

He ate quickly, listening to the radio and the talk of cold weather and fog. Then he got up and took his plate and cup to the kitchen, placing them on the counter. *I'm sure Mary won't mind doing them,* he thought distractedly, looking at the time. *I better just check on Jennet and get going*. He opened the back door and walked down the steps to the stable. Jennet was laying down when Frankie unbolted the

222

doors. 'You all right, Jennet?' Frankie said. Jennet got up and walked over to Frankie at the door. He gave her a rub down the neck and quickly looked her over to make sure she was all right. He checked she had plenty of feed and water and gave her a final pat before shutting up the doors.

Back inside, Frankie checked himself over in the hall mirror, put on his hat and coat and opened the front door. *Well, it will all be over after today*, he thought as he locked the door and climbed into the car. The car still smelled faintly of lavender and of Mary. Frankie started the engine and began driving towards Reading.

After half an hour or so of driving, Frankie found himself in a queue of traffic. *I hope this doesn't last too long*, he thought, *otherwise I could be late*. Three quarters of an hour later, Frankie had only covered about ten miles. *I'm definitely going to be late now.*

Eventually, the traffic started to move but Frankie was now well behind schedule. As the roads cleared, he put his foot down on the accelerator to catch up on time. *Not too fast Frankie, please. Slow down.*

'Of course, dear,' Frankie said. 'I'll get us there safely.'

As he pulled into the carpark in Reading, Frankie was just over an hour late. He quickly parked the car and walked hurriedly into the entrance to the courts, his footsteps echoing loud in the wide corridor. He looked around and saw the Number One Court across the hall. He quietly opened the door and walked in.

'Ah, there you are, Mr Mills,' said a voice to his right. Frankie turned and saw Inspector George Allen waving him over.

Frankie walked across the room to the inspector, who invited him to sit down in the empty seat next to him. 'What happened?' asked the inspector.

'We got stuck in traffic,' replied Frankie.

'We?' said the inspector, glancing behind Frankie. He shrugged. 'Well, we've presented the evidence, such as we have, and the judge has been out to consider it. He'll be back shortly to deliver the verdict. I'm afraid I'm not hopeful.'

'Is that him?' asked Frankie, pointing to a man stood in the dock with a policeman at either side. He was a rough-looking character, tall and burly, with unruly black hair and a fearsome scowl that he was directing at the court officers.

'Yes, that's him,' said the inspector. 'His name is James Smith. He's got a list of crimes a mile long. But I'm afraid it doesn't look good in this case. He's pleaded not guilty throughout and without much evidence we will be lucky to get a full trial.'

The clerk of the court returned and asked everyone to stand. The judge took his place and, after he was seated, everyone else followed except the defendant, who was told to remain standing.

'James Smith, you have a long and colourful record of criminality and from that I am minded for the good of society to allow the prosecutor to consider a full trial,' he paused and glanced out across court. 'However, that is not how the law works. Unfortunately, on this instance, I can only conclude that there is insufficient evidence to proceed to a full trial and, if I were to allow it, there would be insufficient chance of a conviction taking place.

'Mr Smith, against all my better judgement, I have no choice but to consider you not guilty of the crime of murder and you are, therefore, free to go. God have mercy on us all.'

James Smith burst into tears as he left the dock and walked free from the court. Frankie too felt a wave of relief flood through him.

'Damn!' said the inspector, slamming his fist against the railing. 'Well, there you are, Mr Mills. As I suspected, not enough evidence, I'm afraid. We'll continue our search for the person responsible, but without some major breakthrough or some new evidence... well, we will keep trying.'

'Thank you for all your efforts,' said Frankie. 'I really don't know if he was guilty or not, he looked innocent in the dock.'

'Believe me,' said the inspector, 'you never can tell by appearances alone. Even the most learned of police officers can be fooled on occasion. And James Smith is not a good man, not a good man at all.'

Frankie nodded. 'Of course, and you will know better than me. It's just when the defendant was found not guilty, the look on his face made me think he was innocent.'

'Maybe you're right, Mr Mills. We will continue our investigations nevertheless. But, as I said, without the weapon or witnesses, I just don't know.'

The inspector opened the door and led Frankie outside.

They both quickly walked down the road to where they had parked. When they reached the inspector's car, he turned to Frankie and said, 'I apologise again, Mr Mills, but we will continue to search for the person responsible. It's not over yet, so don't give up.'

'Thank you, Inspector,' replied Frankie. 'I appreciate all you've done.'

Frankie returned to his car and climbed in. He took off his hat and placed it on the back seat with his coat. He turned on the engine and then the windscreen wipers as the damp foggy air was now closing in.

The fog thickened further as Frankie drove, yet a feeling of lightness swept through him. It was finally all over, he realised. No more would he worry about blackmailers or innocent men hanging for his crime. No more nightmares or guilt or fear. Angela and Stephen would never need to know what he had done; they were safe from the shame and horror of it all. Shirley and Bobby too would be okay now, safe and provided for, although Frankie realised he would not be able to drop in on his way home as he said he would because the fog meant he was having to drive more slowly. He hoped they would forgive him that little breach of promise. He was sure they would.

Outside, the darkness was closing in around the gossamer fog that enveloped his car. Yet Frankie did not mind.

'Shall we stop anywhere on the way, dearest,' he said aloud.

No, just come home to me now, darling.

Frankie turned and smiled at Mary, looking as beautiful as

226

he had ever remembered her, in her blue-checked dress, her nut-brown hair free around her shoulders. She smiled at him, her eyes sparkling in the light that was getting suddenly brighter.

'I love you, Mary,' said Frankie.

I love you too, and Mary reached out for his hand as the brightness engulfed them both.

Epilogue

Newbury Police Station, 1936

Inspector George Allen was sat down at his desk with a cup of tea in hand. He yawned deeply; it had been a long drive home last night. He had stopped for some dinner after the hearing to avoid the fog, but that had been a mistake. The roads had been awful when he'd finally started home.

There was a knock at his door. George looked up to see Sergeant Dick Henry leaning on the frame. 'Sad news, huh, George?'

'What is?' asked the inspector. 'What's happened?'

***

Stephen pulled in to the hospital car park, finding a space and pulling the handbrake hard before exiting the car. For a second, he forgot to lock it, but then quickly turned back and made the car safe. He was shaking, he knew he was shaking, nerves and sickness combined, he was coughing too. He had not expected to find himself back at the hospital so soon. The doctor would be furious to know he was up and out of bed already, but it was too important. Of course, Angela had offered to go instead, but Stephen could not let her be exposed to that tragedy too. She had been through enough recently, more than enough.

He pulled himself up the steps using the cold, metal rail, to be met by the ashen-faced inspector.

'Mr Sheehan, sorry to see you again under such awful circumstances.'

Stephen nodded, trying to catch his breath. 'Inspector. Thank you for calling me.'

'Well, I knew that you're friends with Mr Mills,' the inspector frowned. 'Are you okay, sir? You look rather unwell.'

Stephen shook his head. 'I'll be fine, Inspector. I just need to get this done. I need to know.'

'Of course.'

Inspector Allen turned and led Stephen through the now familiar hallways, with the familiar scents and sounds, down the stairs to the all too familiar morgue. A body lay on the table covered with a sheet. Breathless from the walk, Stephen felt his stomach churn with apprehension as he stood there, in a place he had never wanted to see again.

'He was a war hero, you know,' said Stephen to the inspector. 'He won the military medal for taking out a gun nest, saving us all. He did so many things back then, saved my life so many times. I met my wife through him too, my children exist because of him. I owe him so much.'

'He seemed a good man.'

Stephen nodded. 'What happened, Inspector?'

Inspector Allen shrugged. 'It was the fog last night. It seems Frankie's car somehow swerved into an oncoming truck. It was quick, he probably wouldn't have known.'

'Is the truck driver okay?' Stephen asked.

The inspector nodded.

'Good,' said Stephen. 'Frankie would hate to have hurt someone else. Shall we do this?'

The inspector gestured to the technician, who pulled back the sheet.

'He looks so peaceful,' said Stephen with a sad smile. 'I haven't seen him so peaceful in a long time.'

Stephen stepped forward towards Frankie and placed a hand on the clammy cold flesh.

'Goodbye, my friend.' He turned to the inspector. 'He's with Mary now, you know. That's all he ever wanted – my friend, Frankie – to be with his Mary. Well, they can be together forever now. Together forever.'

THE END

Acknowledgements

Writing a novel is not easy and I would like to thank everyone who has helped, guided and encouraged me through this long process. In particular, my mother, Shirley Howe, who inspired me to write the book and who gave me ideas and suggestions throughout, and my daughter and her husband, Clare and Mark Tucker, for their technical support, their help, their patience and their encouragement.

Finally, the editors, Charlie Wilson and Angela Stokes, who guided me through the final stages of publishing the book. I want to thank you for all your hard work, your reviews, your thoughts and your ideas. Your wonderful ability to pick an author up when they really need it and encourage confidence when it is lacking has been much appreciated.

I am so thankful to everyone who has supported me in achieving my dream of publishing my very own novel.

About the Author

Stephen Howe was born in Windsor in Royal Berkshire, but grew up in the historic market town of Newbury in West  Berkshire. The eldest of six children, Stephen has always been interested in horses ever since his father asked him to pick out a horse in the Grand National at the age of ten. He put a sixpence each way on it and it won at 50/1.

Stephen's other interests are archaeology and ancient history. He has a passion for metal detecting and has been searching the fields of Berkshire for ancient treasures for forty years. His best find to date is an iron age coin, known as a gold stater, from around 50 B.C.

Stephen has written several stories about his treasure hunting adventures for *Treasure Hunting* and *The Searcher* magazines. He has also written two stories about the lives of some of his ancestors from the eighteenth and early-nineteenth centuries. Stephen was inspired to write *A Wounded Mind*, his first novel, by his mother after he told her about a dream he had about two jockey's riding over the jumps.

Printed in Great Britain
by Amazon

16526566R00136